STORM SURGE

Lantern Beach Mysteries, Book 3

CHRISTY BARRITT

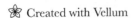

Complete Book List

Squeaky Clean Mysteries:

#1 Hazardous Duty

#2 Suspicious Minds

#2.5 It Came Upon a Midnight Crime (novella)

#3 Organized Grime

#4 Dirty Deeds

#5 The Scum of All Fears

#6 To Love, Honor and Perish

#7 Mucky Streak

#8 Foul Play

#9 Broom & Gloom

#10 Dust and Obey

#11 Thrill Squeaker

#11.5 Swept Away (novella)

#12 Cunning Attractions

#13 Cold Case: Clean Getaway

While You Were Sweeping, A Riley Thomas Spinoff

The Sierra Files:
#1 Pounced
#2 Hunted
#3 Pranced
#4 Rattled
#5 Caged (coming soon)

The Gabby St. Claire Diaries (a Tween Mystery series):
#1 The Curtain Call Caper
#2 The Disappearing Dog Dilemma
#3 The Bungled Bike Burglaries

The Worst Detective Ever
#1 Ready to Fumble
#2 Reign of Error
#3 Safety in Blunders
#4 Join the Flub
#5 Blooper Freak
#6 Flaw Abiding Citizen
#7 Gaffe Out Loud (coming soon)

Raven Remington
#1 Relentless

Holly Anna Paladin Mysteries:
#1 Random Acts of Murder
#2 Random Acts of Deceit
#2.5 Random Acts of Scrooge

The Good Girl

Suspense:
Imperfect
The Wrecking

Standalone Romantic-Suspense:
Keeping Guard
The Last Target
Race Against Time
Ricochet
Key Witness
Lifeline
High-Stakes Holiday Reunion
Desperate Measures
Hidden Agenda
Mountain Hideaway
Dark Harbor
Shadow of Suspicion
The Baby Assignment

Nonfiction:
Characters in the Kitchen
Changed: True Stories of Finding God through Christian Music
The Novel in Me: The Beginner's Guide to Writing and Publishing a Novel

Prologue

CADY MATTHEWS FROZE in the dingy hallway.

The sound of a whiny hum mixed with a faint tapping—so faint that Cady thought she'd imagined it. Yet something about the noise seemed to beckon for attention, to whisper of urgency.

She pivoted in the cold, dim space, the hairs on her arms rising at the chilly undercurrents around her.

The noise came from somewhere in the underbelly of this building. She was in DH-7's lair—an old apartment complex the gang had taken over. It now served as their base of operations—their base of *deadly* operations. She mentally called the building "Hell's Waiting Room." What other name would be appropriate for a building where so much evil occurred?

Nothing. Not in her mind, at least.

Cady, a police detective, was here undercover, but the assignment felt more difficult with each second that ticked by. Truth be told, she wanted out. But the other truth also remained: she wasn't a quitter.

Not with this assignment. And not with that noise she'd just heard.

"What are you doing?" Raul Sanders stepped through an open door a little farther down the hallway and came toward her. Two of his top guys, Sloan and Orion, flanked him on either side.

Cady tried to maintain her aloof behavior, to conceal the fear and repulsion she felt toward the man. She thought she had her act perfected. Usually. Right now, she felt off-balance and not at the top of her game.

"Looking for you, of course," she said.

"Everything okay?"

She nodded. "Yeah, I just wanted to see what you needed me to do."

Cady had—with the help of the entire taskforce behind her integration here—staged it to appear she'd saved his life, and that had fast-tracked her into Raul's inner circle. She reported directly to him.

He studied her face, his lip twitching as he processed some thought unknown to Cady.

She kept her chin up, desperate not to break her cover.

Don't blow it, Cady. Not yet. Just a couple more weeks and you'll have all the information you need to put these guys away for good.

Raul continued to stare at her, his eyes as lifeless as a corpse. Only he wasn't dead. His soul was, though.

"You found us just in time," he finally said. "It's almost time for our Big Easy to be revealed."

"Big Easy? As in New Orleans?" What sense did that make? DH-7 had invaded the entire West Coast, but they operated primarily out of Seattle.

"No, Big Easy as in it's going to make us a lot of easy money." He grinned, his gaze revealing what consumed him. Greed. Power. Lust. "I'll fill you in later."

Cady nodded, wishing he'd tell her now. Wishing she could beg for details and not be in the dark. But she couldn't. Not without showing her hand.

"Later then," she said.

As he walked away, his guys followed—but not before Sloan gave Cady a death glare.

The man didn't like her. He never had.

Even though he and Raul were rarely together, Sloan was Raul's right-hand man. He covered gang operations in California, while Orion covered the Expansion, as Raul called it. That included the gang's spread of influence toward the East. Both men's presence here in Washington state further proved that the gang was planning something big.

She didn't like where things were going, yet she felt powerless to stop it. Right now, at least. There would come a time for everything to fall apart. She knew good and well she could lose her life when that happened.

It was more than she'd signed up for, yet not much in the grand scheme of things. Not when she considered the stakes—those being the safety of the general population at large.

As soon as the men disappeared down the hallway, Cady froze and listened for those telltale sounds again. The inconsistent hum. The teasing tapping. She needed to know what they were. Where they were coming from.

She leaned against the wall, her fingers pressed into the grimy plaster. All she heard was her own heartbeat. She knew she hadn't imagined the earlier noises.

She stepped away then heard it again.

The noise sounded like a soft beat against the wall.

It wasn't the furnace either. The uneven rhythms made her realize . . . a person was making that sound.

Someone trying to send a message? Trying to get someone's attention? Probably.

Cady's gut twisted as she pondered what to do. This being undercover thing wasn't easy . . . especially when she saw horrible things happen, yet couldn't break her cover. As Samuel Stephens, the taskforce leader, always told her . . . Cady had to keep the big picture in mind.

That didn't stop her from following the sound.

She wandered down the dark hallways with the sickly yellow lights overhead. Those bulbs buzzed and only made everything around her feel like a bad dream or like she was a character in a cheap horror flick.

She wouldn't be that lucky. No, this was all too real. And Cady was in too deep now to do anything but complete the assignment.

The sound got louder, and she continued to follow it, her breathing becoming more labored with each step.

She paused outside one of the doors in a far corner of the building. Was this where the noise came from?

It was her best guess.

She glanced to her left down the hallway. Nothing.

Glanced to the right. Nothing.

Other gang members were close. She heard their voices echoing down distant corridors. But they were far enough away that maybe . . .

Swallowing hard, she grabbed the knob.

She'd check it out. See what was on the other side. And then she'd develop her next plan of action.

Just as she twisted the handle, a footstep sounded in the distance.

Cady jerked her head toward the sound. Sloan stood at the end of the hallway, that icy look in his eyes. The six-foot-plus giant was as imposing as they came. His chest, arms, and neck were covered with tattoos, his ears and eyebrows were pierced multiple times, and his hair had been shaved to the scalp.

"What are you doing?" He reached her with quick strides, gripped her wrist, and twisted it until Cady gasped.

"Nothing." She sucked in another gasp of air, unable to conceal her pain. "I'm not doing nothing."

"Could have fooled me," he growled, twisting her arm again until it felt like it might snap. "You need to mind your own business."

"I am." Was this how it all would end? It couldn't. Not until Cady found what she needed to make this all worth it. If she died now, her work would be in vain.

Sloan leaned close, so close that she could smell cigarettes, halitosis, and coffee. "I don't like you. I don't know what it is, but I don't trust you like Raul does. The only reason you're still here is because Raul insists that you're good enough to rise in the ranks one day."

She shivered—both at his words and at the thought of remaining in DH-7 any longer than necessary. She couldn't imagine being the mastermind behind their deadly schemes. Couldn't fathom immersing herself any more deeply in the dark, vicious world that stole people's souls as easily as a skilled pickpocket stole wallets on a busy street corner.

She jerked away from Sloan's grasp, careful to keep the defiant look on her face—a look she'd perfected for her cover. "I need to go."

"You do that. But I'm watching you."

That was going to be a problem. Because Cady really wanted to know what was in that room. She wouldn't be finding out right now, though.

Chapter One

TODAY'S GOALS: CONTINUE LIFE AS NORMAL. SELL
ICE CREAM. COOL IT WITH THE GOOGLE SEARCHES.

AS HAD BECOME HER ROUTINE, Cassidy
Livingston stepped onto her deck just as the sun rose
over the roaring Atlantic. She couldn't imagine not
drinking in this view one day. The peacefulness of it
helped her clear her head, gain her focus, and remind
herself of her alternate personality.

Cady Matthews from Seattle, Washington, was
gone. Cassidy Livingston of Lantern Beach, North
Carolina, had taken her place.

Her old life seemed so far away from this island,
where the sand had not only invaded her pores but
her heart as well.

Cassidy had been on this isolated island for two
months. She had four more to go. In some ways, that
seemed like an eternity and in others it wasn't long
enough.

Time shows us what's important.

She'd just been pondering that inspirational quote earlier, a nugget of wisdom from an old Day-at-a-Glance calendar that used to belong to her best friend, Lucy. The wisdom never ceased to be useful and relevant—especially since Cassidy came here to Lantern Beach.

"It's beautiful, isn't it, Kujo?" She glanced down at the golden retriever sitting beside her. He belonged to her neighbor Ty Chambers, but Cassidy was dog-sitting while Ty was out of town.

The dog nuzzled her hand in response.

"Days should start with pondering how big the world is and how small you are in comparison, right, boy?"

He barked in affirmation.

Cassidy took another sip of her coffee. As she scanned the shoreline, she paused and squinted. What was that?

Some kind of object had been beached a little farther down the sandy banks. From her perch atop her second-level deck, she couldn't make out any details, except that it appeared to be rectangular with blue and black tarps covering the edges.

She set her coffee on the railing, climbed down her exterior stairway, and trod over a patch of sandy cement before reaching the small path that cut over the dunes toward the beach.

As she passed Ty's house, she glanced over. He'd been out of town for six days, but Cassidy suspected he was home now. She'd seen a light on in one of his windows last night. It was hard to know for sure, since he hadn't taken his truck with him. Apparently, an old friend had picked him up.

A surprising jolt of sadness diced through her heart at the realization that he hadn't called. Their relationship was strange, one where they took two steps forward and one step back. But Cassidy had thought he'd call. Or stay in touch. Or do something to indicate he cared.

But the truth was, it was better this way. Ty had broken down her walls, and she'd been in the process of trying to restore them. Ty didn't know who Cassidy really was, and when he found out . . . she had no idea what he would think.

Car tires rumbled behind her, and Cassidy paused. A moment later, Serena Lavinia jumped out of her rundown Ford Fiesta and rushed toward Cassidy. Today, the woman-of-many-faces was dressed like a preppy boarding-school girl in a button-up top and khaki shorts. Serena always kept Cassidy on her toes with her ever-changing personalities. The girl took "finding herself" to a whole new level.

Cassidy motioned for Serena to join her on the narrow path to the beach. As she crested the dune, a strong breeze hit her. Even when it was 90 outside, this breeze made it feel 20 degrees cooler. That worked out well in the summer, but she couldn't imagine the place during winter.

"I was hoping I'd catch you," Serena said, joining

her on the sand. "I wanted to ask if I could take an earlier shift today."

"Why's that?" Cassidy kept walking, and Serena joined her.

"I have a story to cover later for the paper, and the person I need to interview is only available at three. It's the organizer of the Fourth of July parade."

Fourth of July was three days away, and apparently Lantern Beach liked to celebrate big. There was not only a parade here on the tiny island, but also concerts by local musicians and church groups, an art show, and even a 5K.

"That is exciting." Cassidy said. "I'm glad you're enjoying all your jobs so much."

Serena worked part-time for Cassidy, part-time at her aunt Skye's produce stand, and part-time as a beat reporter for the local island newspaper.

"So . . . about the shifts?" Serena asked, raking her dark hair from her eyes as the wind hit her.

"I don't mind if we switch," Cassidy answered.

It wasn't like Cassidy had anything better to do on the island, a fact that normally drove her crazy. For as long as she could remember, her whole life had been filled with purpose, and to-do lists, and twelve-step plans on how to move ahead. She'd always been an over-achiever, and it was eye-opening trying to simply be an ice cream woman now.

Cassidy glanced again at the mystery object, which was only eight feet away now. What could that be? Something from a ship? A temporary shelter that had blown down the beach? Part of Blackbeard's treasure?

As she reached the structure, she saw it was six feet long and three feet wide. Was that a boat? Maybe a raft some kids had made? She had trouble picturing children putting this together. The vessel was too . . . complex.

Her gut churned. There was more to this. An ominous feeling hovered over her as she peered above the edge.

"What is this?" Serena wrinkled her nose at what looked to be a pile of trash.

Cassidy squinted. "That's what I'm trying to figure out."

"It looks like a boat."

"It does, doesn't it?" Cassidy continued to stare at the wreckage. She felt sure that's what it was—something the ocean had eaten up and spit back out.

The sides of the structure were comprised of Styrofoam that had been duct-taped in place. The frame was some sort of metal. Bottles and snack wrappers littered the bottom of the craft.

Her apprehension churned harder.

"This is crazy," Serena said, jiggling the side. "But it's pretty sturdy."

Cassidy picked up something inside. She sucked in a breath at what she saw.

It was a cloth. And it was bloody.

People had been on this contraption. People who were hurt or injured.

This hadn't been a peaceful adventure. No, this had been a life-or-death mission.

Cassidy pulled out her phone. She needed to call the police. Now.

Chapter Two

"I'VE SEEN this type of craft before," police chief Alan Bozeman said. "It's from Cuba."

"Cuba?" Cassidy stared at the chief, using her hand to block the glare of the sun coming off the ocean.

She had little to no confidence in the man, and nothing he'd done since Cassidy arrived in town had proven that she should put her trust in him. Bozeman seemed to bumble one investigation after the other, earning him the nickname among locals of Chief Bozoman.

Cassidy had learned a couple weeks back that he'd mostly gotten the job because his father was a state senator. Bozeman didn't even look like someone who was serious about law enforcement with his oversized belly and shifty gaze.

Bozeman nodded as they stood on the sand, the offshore breeze slapping them and its force turning their clothing into something that looked shrink-wrapped around them. "That's right. Cuba. Must have gotten sucked up in the current. The storm surge from that tropical depression that's been churning out in the Atlantic is crazy strong. Red flags are up all along the beach. Vacationers aren't very happy about it."

If that was true, then . . . "Where are the people who were inside?"

"We'll probably never know. They walk among us." Bozeman laughed, but the sound trailed off when he realized no one else was joining in.

"So you're saying some refugees from Cuba were in this raft that the jet stream propelled up here, and now whoever was onboard is gone?" Cassidy repeated what he'd said to make sure she understood Bozeman's theory. "And possibly injured?"

The chief looked into the distance a moment before nodding. "Yep, that's what I'm saying. Happened up in Hatteras last year. Apparently, it happens quite often down in Florida. That amount of blood doesn't indicate anything life-threatening, nothing to really worry about."

Cassidy wasn't buying it. There was a story behind this contraption, and she wanted to know what.

She cleared her throat, trying to be subtle and unassuming. "If this is from Cuba, why are there American snacks on board? Fritos? Dasani? Wouldn't there be more things written in Spanish?"

The chief cringed, the blank look in his eyes indicating he didn't really know. "Not necessarily. Everyone wants to be an American, right? Or maybe the occupants picked up some food and drinks along the way."

That was all fine and dandy, but . . . "If they made it to land somewhere in the US they would have just stayed . . . don't you think? What reason could they possibly have for buying food and setting themselves adrift again?" She threw in the "don't you think?" part in an effort to remember her cover as a civilian. It was so hard sometimes.

"Who knows what people like that are thinking?"

"People like that?" Outrage lined Serena's voice. "You mean people who are terrified and desperate?"

The chief cringed, obviously not well-versed on being politically correct. "I'll call in the Coast Guard just to be sure. But I don't think there's anything to worry about."

Of course he didn't.

But Serena was right. Whoever had been aboard this contraption had been desperate.

"I'll take over from here, ladies," the chief said, effectively dismissing them from the scene. "Thanks for calling this in."

Cassidy didn't want to leave the boat, but she had no good excuse to stay. If only she had a moment to inspect the vessel more. To search for more clues. To maybe take some more pictures—she'd snapped a few before the chief arrived.

Low profile and laid-back.

Yep, those attributes were supposed to be Cassidy's middle names since she'd arrived here in Lantern Beach. So far, she'd failed at staying true to either, but she was determined to change that before she drew too much attention to herself.

She, Serena, and Kujo started back toward her cottage, the midsummer sun beating down on them with the force of an oven ripe for roasting as soon as they breached the other side of the dune. Today was trash day, and, when the wind shifted, the rotting odor of curbside cans that hadn't been emptied for a week drifted toward them.

"So about switching my shift . . ." Serena said once they reached the shade under Cassidy's house. "You did say okay, didn't you?"

"Sure, that's fine, Serena." Cassidy was too preoccupied to argue.

The twenty-one-year-old smiled. "Great. Thanks so much!"

Serena scurried off toward Elsa, the pink ice cream truck with a mind of its own. At random times, the vehicle started to play music. Was it an ode to the fact that locals refused to eat any of the treats inside?

Some might claim it was. Thankfully, Cassidy wasn't as superstitious about the fact that the previous owner had been found dead inside—by natural causes, supposedly.

Cassidy watched as Serena climbed into the driver's seat. The college student definitely made

Cassidy's life more interesting with her experiments in discovering herself.

"Hey, Cassidy," Serena called, sticking her head out the back of the truck.

Cassidy paused by the stairs leading up to her place. "What's up?"

"I think someone got into your ice cream truck last night. You might want to come check this out."

Cassidy walked over toward Elsa, anxious to see what Serena was talking about. "Why do you think that?"

"I mean, I don't keep track of inventory or anything, but you don't usually leave things open and wrappers on the floor." Serena scooted back far enough for Cassidy to see the mess in the back of the truck.

Cassidy stuck her head through the door. Sure enough, someone had raided the truck last night. Wrappers were strewn on the floor, brown and white blobs had melted on the small countertop, and a couple of water bottles had been crushed and left behind as well.

Even though Cassidy had secured Elsa last night, it wouldn't surprise her if the locks had suddenly failed, thus allowing some local kids to stock up on free treats. This truck was one malfunction after another.

"How much is gone?" Cassidy craned her neck, trying to see inside the freezer.

Serena peered inside the glass top. "It's hard to

say. But there's definitely stuff missing, especially the drinks and chips we just started selling."

That had been Serena's idea, and the products had been a surprising hit with beachgoers who wanted refreshments other than ice cream after the beach. With no chain grocery stores or fast food restaurants on the island, treats were at a premium—especially ones conveniently obtained.

"I guess I'll need to keep an eye on this in the future," Cassidy said with a frown. She wouldn't report this to the police. She didn't want to draw any more attention to herself than necessary.

But if someone had been down here, why hadn't Cassidy heard anything? She almost always slept with one eye and ear open. When there was a million-dollar bounty on your head, you never fully relaxed.

And wouldn't Kujo have heard something and alerted her?

Cassidy shrugged it off. Maybe she'd been especially tired last night. She had played volleyball with some friends until almost nine o'clock. And the sun had been scorching, which exhausted Cassidy more than she wanted to admit.

"I'll do my best to sell what's left. See you in a few hours!" Serena waved as she pulled away, ready to begin the morning route.

As Cassidy paused on her driveway, Kujo began barking at her incessantly.

"What is it, boy?" Cassidy asked.

He continued to bark, something obviously on his mind.

Cassidy leaned down and lowered her voice. "Did little Timmy fall down a well?"

He barked again.

Cassidy's eyes went to Ty's place. Did Kujo know his owner was home? Did the dog sense Ty's presence?

A growing sense of unease brewed in her stomach. Why wouldn't Ty have told her he was home? Or what if he wasn't home? What if someone had broken into his place and been dumb enough to turn a light on?

She patted the golden retriever's head, her mind made up. "Okay, boy. Let's go check it out."

She climbed the steps to Ty's place. She'd make sure everything was okay and then resume her day as planned. No harm in that, right?

Kujo's barking became more incessant when they reached Ty's door.

Dogs could sense things. What was Kujo's intuition telling him now?

Cassidy checked the lock. The door didn't budge.

Cupping her hands around her eyes, she peered through one of the glass panes on the top half of the door.

Her gaze hit the kitchen first. It looked fine. Then the dining room. Also fine.

She scanned over into the living area, ready to give up and mark this as a fluke.

But what she saw made her pause.

Were those legs?

On the floor?

She darted to another window for a better look, Kujo's barks urging her to continue—quickly.

Shading her eyes against the glare of the sun, Ty's living area came into view.

Yes, those were legs. Feet.

Ty's legs and feet.

He was sprawled on the floor, not moving.

Chapter Three

PANIC SURGED THROUGH CASSIDY. She had to get to Ty. Now.

Kujo's barks came more rapidly, followed by a howl that made her shiver. Certainly that sound didn't mean . . . no, it meant nothing. Only distress.

"I know, I know. I hear you, boy," she murmured.

She glanced around and found a block of wood Ty had been using for one of his whittling projects. She rammed it into a panel above the doorknob.

The glass shattered.

She stripped off her button-up shirt—she wore a tank top underneath—and wrapped the shirt around her hand. Carefully—but quickly—she broke the remaining glass from around the windowpane.

Reaching inside, she unlocked the door and opened it. As soon as she did, Kujo rushed ahead of her, reaching his owner and licking his face.

Cassidy dashed behind Kujo toward Ty and knelt

beside him. Her hand went to his neck, searching for a pulse. She held her breath until she felt a rapid *thump, thump*.

It was there.

But it was fast. Too fast.

Cassidy grabbed her cell phone from her back pocket and called 911. Ty needed more help than she could give him, and he needed it now.

After dispatch assured her help was on the way, Cassidy leaned down. "Ty? Can you hear me?"

He let out a low moan.

Her hand went to Ty's forehead. He was burning up. Sweat covered his forehead. His skin looked sickly and pale.

Cassidy scanned the length of him, noting the white T-shirt he wore. His favorite jeans. Her eyes stopping on the bandage at his shoulder.

Bandage?

What . . . what in the world had happened to him?

She patted his cheek, desperate to keep him lucid. "Ty, can you hear me? Can you say something?"

Again, he moaned, and his eyes remained closed.

Dear Lord. I know we're kind of new at this talking thing —really new, actually— but . . . please help him.

In the short time Cassidy had known Ty, he'd come to mean a lot to her. And she was so used to seeing him strong and tough, just like the Navy SEAL he'd been. This side of him . . . it unnerved her.

The ambulance had to get here in time. *Please . . .*

"Ty, you're going to be okay," she whispered, resting a hand against his scruffy cheek and jaw. "I need someone to aggravate. You can't leave me."

At once, his eyes popped open. But the look emanating from his gaze was halfway crazed and totally out of it. His hand darted toward hers.

"Cassidy . . ." he mumbled. His grip on her hand tightened with enough strength that Cassidy squirmed.

She leaned closer, her throat clenched so tightly she could hardly breathe. "I'm here, Ty. Help is on the way."

"Cassidy . . ." His chest rose and fell in a labored motion—like it took too much effort.

Her throat tightened even more. What had happened to him? How long had he been like this?

"Cassidy . . ." he whispered. "I . . . I love you."

Her eyes widened. The man was definitely delusional and not in his right mind. Sure, they had kissed. And he had kissed her like he meant it, for that matter. Her toes had even curled.

But they were nowhere close to being in love.

"Now you're talking crazy," she whispered, thankful to hear the distant cry of sirens.

He shook his head, his eyes gaining a strange focus. "Crazy . . . for you."

His fever had made him lose all common sense. Just wait until he got better, and Cassidy could give him a hard time about this.

Because he was going to get better . . . right?

"Well, you're crazy all right." Moisture filled Cassidy's eyes. "You have a lot of explaining to do when you get better, Tyson Dylan Chambers. You told me you were going out of town to do something for Hope House. The pieces aren't fitting together right now."

Hope House was the retreat center he was trying to start for veterans dealing with PTSD.

His eyes closed again, causing her heart to hitch. No! He needed to stay alert.

She patted his cheek again. "Ty, stay with me. Help is on the way." The sirens were louder. Closer. Almost here.

"I . . ." His voice faded. His eyes fluttered open and then closed again.

Someone knocked at the door behind her. "Paramedics."

They burst through the door, prodded Cassidy out of the way, and took over.

But Cassidy felt like a piece of her heart had been left with Ty.

A desperate piece.

What if Ty didn't make it out of this alive?

The thought was too much to handle.

Cassidy sat in a stiff chair in the waiting area of the island's one and only medical clinic. The place was small—smaller than her doctor's office back in Seattle.

If she understood correctly, the staff here could accept a limited number of overnight patients, and they had a triage area for minor emergencies.

The next closest hospital would be up in Nags Head, but someone would have to take two ferries to get there, not to mention the sixty-mile drive afterward. With one doctor and three nurses, this was sufficient for anything non-life-threatening.

The place wasn't anything fancy, and everything was outdated by at least twenty years. That seemed to be a theme here on the island. The waiting area had been decorated with some red, white, and blue tinsel strung up near the ceiling. Little American flag gels, mixed with some stars, were placed haphazardly on the windows behind her.

But none of that mattered right now. All that mattered was Ty.

As the paramedics had worked on him, Cassidy spotted a bottle of pain pills and a sling on the table beside his couch. By all appearances, he had been to the doctor. Had he had a procedure of some sort? Surgery?

Cassidy sighed and leaned back in her chair. As a detective, she'd been in waiting rooms many times before. But waiting for a status update on someone she cared about . . . it was just painful. Each minute felt like an hour.

Her phone buzzed. She looked down and saw she'd gotten a text from Ty's mom, Del. The woman texted Cassidy at least a few times a week.

Day one of chemo. Pray for me.

Cassidy closed her eyes. Chemo.

This was Del's third battle with cancer. They'd been hoping for a better report, but they hadn't gotten one.

Cassidy had known the woman only a few short weeks, but Del had made her feel like one of the family. And there was a lot to be said for that.

Should she tell Del about Ty?

No, she decided. Until Cassidy knew for sure what was going on, there was no need to stress Del out any more than necessary. Instead she typed:

You're in my prayers. Always.

She glanced up as someone walked into the waiting area. Austin Brooks, one of Ty's best friends, was here.

The man worked construction and looked like he could have stepped from the screen of any home improvement TV show with his wavy dark hair and fit build. Cassidy hadn't called the whole gang, a hodge-podge of people who had met at Bible study. Only Austin, since Ty seemed closest to him.

Austin sat beside Cassidy, tension radiating from him as well as the faint scent of sawdust. "Thanks for letting me know what happened. Any updates?"

Cassidy shook her head. "No, I haven't heard anything yet. I may need you to fix his front door. I had to break out a piece of glass to get inside."

Maybe it was an odd time to mention it, but the

subject seemed safe and the answer certain. Certainty was a comfort at the moment.

"I'd be happy to fix that," Austin said. "Do you have any idea what exactly is wrong with Ty?"

"No clue. Kujo just kept barking at his house this morning, so I went to check it out. That's when I found him."

The memory felt surreal and caused Cassidy to flinch as a dull, achy pain filled her chest cavity.

"I can't believe he didn't tell us he was back." Austin ran a hand through his hair. "I wonder who even gave him a ride here."

Cassidy straightened. There was more to this story than she realized—more than Ty had shared with her. "What happened to his shoulder, Austin?"

"He had surgery."

Cassidy shook her head quickly, uncertain if she'd heard correctly. "Wait . . . he told you he was having surgery?"

Austin turned to look at her, wrinkles of confusion at the edges of his eyes. "I thought you knew."

"No, Ty told me he was out of town, doing some stuff for Hope House. He never mentioned anything about surgery."

Austin frowned, leaning forward with his elbows propped on his legs. "Yeah, sorry. I'm not really sure why he'd keep it quiet. He had shoulder surgery and then went to rehab for several days. Said it was no big deal. I gave him a ride to the hospital in Raleigh. I figured he'd call me when he was ready to come home."

An uncertain emotion roiled in Cassidy's stomach. Why would Ty keep this from her? It made no sense. They were . . . friends. Ty had said he wanted to be even more. So why . . .

"Sorry," Austin said again. "He hasn't been acting like himself the past few weeks. I figured between the news about his mom's cancer and the fact that he hasn't been raising the funding for his project like he hoped, he was just in a funk."

"It would make sense." Cassidy had thought she was the one who'd put up walls. This whole time Ty had obviously been putting up barriers himself.

Guilt pounded at her. It was a familiar emotion lately, and one she didn't like.

"What kind of surgery?" Cassidy asked.

"Shoulder. Bone spur, I think. Maybe an impingement? He wasn't exactly clear. Either way, it was an old injury from his days as a SEAL. I guess he aggravated it a couple weeks back."

Had that happened when he'd rescued Cassidy and Skye?

More guilt filled her.

"I heard the surgery went well," Austin continued. "The doctor expected recovery time to be minimal. Ty even went to some special rehab therapy place for a few days. They're supposed to whip you in shape in half the time."

"Sounds unlikely . . . but great if it works."

She glanced in the distance and saw a door open. Her heart quickened. Doc Clemson had stepped into the room. The man, who also served as the town's medical examiner, had yellowish-orange hair and an easy laugh.

Except for now. Now he looked serious.

Cassidy stood, anxious to hear what he had to say, and met him halfway across the room. Austin followed.

"He's going to be okay," the doctor started.

The air *whooshed* from Cassidy's lungs. Thank goodness.

"It's going to take a while for the antibiotics to kick in," Doc Clemson continued. "It looks like an infection set in at the site of his surgery. It's a good thing you found him when you did because his fever was dangerously high. It must have developed overnight. This could have easily turned into sepsis."

At least she could be thankful for that.

"Can we see him?" Austin stood beside Cassidy, his hands on his hips.

"Not yet. He needs to rest, and we gave him a sedative to help him do so. But I'll have my nurse call you when he wakes up."

"He's . . . he's going to be okay?" Cassidy hated how weak the inquiry made her sound. And the doctor had already answered that question. She just needed to hear it again.

"It looks like he's going to be fine, but we're going to monitor him. He should be okay here at the clinic.

If anything changes, we'll take him to the hospital up in Nags Head. I've already talked to his surgeon, and we're both on the same page."

Cassidy pointed behind her. "Maybe I should just wait . . ."

"There's no need," Doc Clemson said, his frown larger than the average person's as his sagging skin folded around it. "The island is small. I'll call you when it's time, and you can be here in ten minutes. You're just going to go crazy if you sit around here. Our snack machine is even broken, so you'll go hungry too. And the coffee can easily be mistaken for toilet water."

"He's right," Austin said. "Ty is going to be so doped up, he's not going to know what's going on. He wouldn't want us to see him like that."

Except she already had, and Ty had told Cassidy he loved her. Certainly he hadn't meant the words.

Cassidy knew he didn't. Then why had hearing him utter the phrase brought her a burst of joy?

Reluctantly, Cassidy nodded in agreement with Austin and the doc. Maybe she'd go see if the raft had been hauled away yet. By the time she did that, maybe Ty would be awake, and he could clear up some things for her.

She could hope. She could pray. As a matter of fact, she'd do both.

Chapter Four

CASSIDY GATHERED her thoughts in the privacy of her car as she sat outside the clinic.

She pulled out her phone and found a picture Del had sent her—a picture she'd taken of Cassidy and Ty faking a kiss. Well, the kiss had been real. But their relationship hadn't. Long story.

Still, Cassidy couldn't bring herself to delete the photo. It was not only beautiful with the sunset smearing the sky around them with lovely shades of pastel blues, oranges, and pinks. But seeing her and Ty smiling with their arms around each other still made Cassidy feel warm and gooey inside.

Ty Chambers did something to her that no one else ever had. She'd had plenty of boyfriends before. She'd dated plenty of guys. But never anyone like Ty, someone who was masculine yet kind. Who was tough but generous. Who was brave but honorable.

Seeing him like she had today . . . it shook her to

the core. She hadn't, until this moment, realized just how deeply she cared for him.

But that didn't mean anything. It *couldn't* mean anything—anything except that she'd found a friend in him. To ask for anything beyond that would be irrational, especially since she was on borrowed time here.

Her phone beeped in her purse.

Her secret phone.

She quickly found it. There were only two people who could call her on this number—and that meant she needed to answer pronto because both signified something important had happened.

Her heart slowed a bit when she saw Samuel Stephens's name there. "What's going on?"

"Good day to you too." His deep but dry voice sounded comfortingly familiar. "But you have the right idea. We should skip the pleasantries. Someone else is dead."

Her headed pounded at his words. "What do you mean?"

"A woman in Dallas. She looked like you. Like the old you. Authorities believe that a member of DH-7 is behind the crime, and that this person thought they'd found you."

Her head pounded harder. A million-dollar bounty on Cassidy's head gave people a lot of incentive—incentive for murder.

But someone else had already died—a woman in San Diego. The gang had made it clear they were out for Cassidy's blood and that innocent lives would be collateral damage—without apology.

"Oh, Samuel . . ." She squeezed the skin between her eyes and let the AC blow on her cheeks.

"We're working on it," he said. "I didn't want you to find out online. That's why I called to tell you myself. It's not your fault, Cassidy."

"It feels like it is." As did Ty's latest injury and surgery.

"I'm sure they're hoping to shake you out by doing things like this."

He was right but . . . "Those poor women."

"Believe me, we're all mourning what's happened" He paused. "Listen, I don't have much time. I also wanted to let you know that DBS News is hunting around for a story on this."

Cassidy's guilt turned to alarm. A national news story on what had happened? That could only spell trouble.

"The gang doesn't need any publicity," she said.

"Of course, the media isn't wording it as publicity, per se. They say they want to bring attention to the woman who bravely killed a notorious gang leader. This underground following of Commotio Cordis doesn't help matters. People think of you as a superhero."

Commotio cordis was the medical term for what had happened when a person's heart stopped after a hard impact. Cassidy had thrown a baseball at Raul's chest, effectively—and unintentionally—killing him.

35

"I never set out to be one." Nor did she feel like one, for that matter.

"I know that. But public interest is high. I've told all my guys not to speak to the press. But Ryan Samson seems to believe the publicity would be good."

Ryan? Cassidy's breath caught when she heard his name. Before she'd come to Lantern Beach, she'd thought she was going to marry the man. Then he'd stopped returning her phone calls, and she'd had to break up with him via voicemail.

It was so obvious now that the man didn't care about her. Cassidy had been a fool to ever think so.

"What did you tell him?" she asked.

"I told him it was a bad idea. But he has a mind of his own, as I'm sure you know."

"All he's concerned about is being elected as pros-ecuting attorney for King County."

"You'll get no argument from me about that." Samuel paused. "Stay safe, Cassidy. There are a lot of rumblings with DH-7."

"What kind?"

"They're desperate to find you and will stop at nothing. You only need to make it a few more months. I know you must feel alone out there."

The strange thing was that she didn't. In fact, she felt more at home than ever here in Lantern Beach.

Cassidy pulled up to her house a few minutes later, let Kujo out, and walked with him toward the beach.

She leaned down and rubbed his ears. The dog knew something was wrong with Ty, didn't he? He didn't seem as perky as usual.

"It's going to be okay, buddy," she murmured. "I promise."

He nuzzled against her hand in response.

Her feet hit the sand, and she could feel the heat sizzling beneath her. The sand got scorching hot, especially on days like today when the temperature soared into the high 90s.

She pulled off her long-sleeved shirt—she'd put it back on at the clinic—and tied it around her waist. Wearing a tank top beneath everything had become a way of life since she'd moved here. The AC inside businesses felt like a freezer and the heat outside like an oven, making for some challenges when it came to dressing. She'd learned layering was the best option.

She paused just over the sand dune and scanned the shoreline. Numerous groups had set up for a day on the shore. Umbrellas and colorful towels lined the beach. However, the riptide kept people from the water, and the tumultuous storm surge stole half of the shoreline.

But the raft was gone.

Already.

That was fast.

She glanced at her watch.

Or maybe not. She *had* been gone three hours

already.

"If it isn't Jessica Fletcher meets Lara Croft," a familiar voice sounded behind her.

She turned and smiled at the friendly face approaching. "Hey, Mac. Fancy seeing you here."

Mac was the town's former police chief. The man was spry with thinning white hair and a matching beard and mustache. He'd become one of Cassidy's favorite people since she'd come here. He was always full of stories dotted with dry humor and had a commentary about life on Lantern Beach that was uniquely his own.

He might be in his late sixties, but the man was sharp and constantly kept up his skills as a law enforcement officer.

"I decided to come fishing," he said, tugging at the floppy hat on his head, one that matched the vest across his chest.

But there was one thing missing. "No fishing pole?"

His eyes sparkled. "I knew I forgot something."

"You see the raft?"

He shrugged and lowered himself atop the sand dune. "I hung out while they loaded the boat up and had it towed to the station. Then I heard about Ty. Thought I'd wait around till you got back and see what was going on."

Cassidy sat beside him, watching as Kujo chased off some seagulls, and she gave the former police chief the update.

"Ty's one stubborn man," Mac said. "It's what made him a good SEAL."

"I suppose." Cassidy knew his words were true, but Ty's stubbornness could have landed him in the hospital with something more serious—something deadly.

Cassidy was thankful she'd stopped by when she had.

Mac squeezed her shoulder and gave her a little shake. "He's tough, Cassidy. He'll come through this."

Cassidy didn't realize that how much this scare had shaken her was so obvious. She pulled back her emotions and let out a sigh. Getting close to the people here was *not* a part of her plan.

But it was like she'd been telling herself—she wasn't the same person now as she'd been before she came here. Her time undercover had changed her. She hoped it was for the best.

She straightened, realizing she was being entirely too transparent. In her current situation, transparency was dangerous. "Thanks, Mac. Now, about that raft. Any updates, other than the fact they had it was towed to the police station?"

"The Coast Guard will probably check it out."

"And then what?"

He shrugged, staring at the ocean and throwing some broken shells from the dune closer to the water. "My guess? They'll probably dispose of it."

"Really? That seems . . . I don't know. Like it's not very thorough."

"I suppose there's no crime in making a raft and setting adrift."

"But there's a story there."

"Oh, I know that. But we'll probably never figure out who was in that raft. We have no clue if they're in this area. They could have been tossed overboard. They could have swam to shore thirty miles south of here. And without any evidence of a crime . . ."

"There was a bloody cloth inside . . ." Cassidy reminded him.

His eyebrows shot up in surprise. "Was there? Now, that's the first I've heard of that."

A sound in the distance caught Cassidy's ear. Elsa. She'd recognize those electronic chimes anywhere. Serena must be hitting the area near here now.

Cassidy absently brushed some sand from her legs. "The chief seemed to indicate that there was a clear Cuba connection."

"You don't think so?"

Cassidy tried to temper her words. "Not that I know anything about this. But . . ."

"Don't sell yourself short."

Kujo wandered back over, and Cassidy gave him another head rub. "Well, everything inside the raft looked American. I would expect if the occupants had departed from Cuba that the food items I saw would have Spanish labels."

"That, my dear, is an excellent point. But the like-lihood we'll find answers? It's not strong."

"I know that's true. I just can't help but think that

whoever was onboard that raft . . . they were desperate. Really desperate."

Just then, her cell phone buzzed. It was the clinic. Cassidy sucked in a quick breath of anticipation.

"I've got to take this," she told Mac before putting the phone to her ear.

"Ty's awake, and he's asking for you," a nurse said.

"I'll be right there." Cassidy turned back to Mac. "I need to go."

"Why don't you let good old Kujo hang out with me for a while?" Mac said. "He looks like he could use some company too."

The dog did appear to be downcast since they'd found Ty. His gait didn't seem as perky, nor did his pant. "That's a great idea. You don't mind?"

"Not at all. Maybe I could use the company too. Besides, I want to brush up on my canine training skills, and I think Kujo would be an excellent student for scouting out scents."

She stood and brushed the sand from her legs again, not even fazed by Mac's "training" anymore. She'd already seen him rappelling down the side of his house and trying to defuse a fake bomb. Nothing wrong with someone trying to keep their skill set fresh.

"Thanks, Mac."

"It's no problem. Keep me updated."

"I will." Cassidy rushed to her car and headed back to the clinic.

Chapter Five

CASSIDY ARRIVED at the clinic ten minutes later, just as Doc Clemson had predicted, and rushed inside.

A pleasant nurse behind the front desk smiled at her. "Go on in."

Despite her hurry, Cassidy paused outside Ty's door, trying to compose herself before she saw him. She shoved a hair behind her ear, drew in a deep breath, and finally stepped inside.

All her composure disappeared when she spotted Ty in the hospital bed, an IV dripping beside him, and an ugly green hospital gown draped over his broad chest. His dark hair usually had a messy vibe to it, but right now it looked flat, and his normally sun-kissed skin was still pale. Even though he was awake, his eyes still looked hazy and glazed.

She strode toward him, pausing by his bed to take his hand. A faint smile crossed his lips, gone just as quickly as it appeared.

"Hey," he muttered.

"You gave me a good scare."

"I'm sorry."

She swallowed back the lump of emotions in her throat. She preferred Ty strong and healthy, but she was so immensely happy he was okay. "How are you?"

"Been better." His eyelids drooped, and Cassidy would bet he was on pain medication in addition to the antibiotics.

She wanted to fuss at him. Desperately wanted to give him a piece of her mind for keeping secrets. For not trusting her. For being so foolish.

Then again, who was she to talk?

"Hey." Ty squeezed her hand.

Cassidy drew her eyes up to his, realizing she'd disappeared for a moment into a sea of self-doubt. "Yes?"

"Thank you." His voice cracked, and he licked his lips.

She grabbed the cup of water from a tray beside her and raised it to his mouth. He took a sip, and Cassidy set it back on the tray.

"What did the doctor say?" Cassidy sat in a metal chair by the bed, after pulling it even closer. Her pulse quickened as she waited for his answer. Even though she'd already talked to Doc Clemson, part of her feared an update she hadn't seen coming.

"That I'll be okay. I'll have to stay for a few days

so he can monitor me. It was either that, or he was going to send me back to Raleigh."

Cassidy stared at Ty a minute, stared at the perfect lines on his face. Not perfect because he was picture perfect—though he was close—but perfect because the man was becoming a fixture in her life. Perfect because she'd stared into those eyes and felt waves of comfort come over her. Because those lips had assured her of protection and help, and he hadn't let her down. That was something Cassidy couldn't say about many people.

"Why didn't you tell me, Ty?" Her voice sounded hoarse. "I could have helped."

He shrugged, his head falling to the side as if all his energy was gone. "I didn't want to bother you."

"I'm your friend. It wouldn't have been a bother. I know Austin feels the same way, and I'd imagine the rest of the gang does also."

Ty pressed his lips together, as if formulating his words. "I suppose that sometimes I have more pride than I should. I thought I could handle it all and that I didn't have to worry or inconvenience anyone. I guess I was wrong."

He was always so busy worrying about others . . . it was one more thing to love and hate about him.

She shifted into teasing mode, sensing Ty's exhaustion and not wanting to wear him out with her questions, which could easily turn into something resembling an interrogation.

"Well, if you pull another stunt like this while I'm

here in town, I'll make it a point to only feed you ice cream from Elsa while you're in recovery," she said. "Mark my words."

"You'll fully embrace being Nurse Ratched, huh?" He chuckled but it faded quickly. "I'll keep that in mind. Might be good incentive."

"I thought so."

Ty's probing gaze latched onto hers. "While you're in in town?"

Cassidy's heart had squeezed when those words had left her lips. "The original plan was to stay only a few months."

"And is that still the plan?"

Her heart pounded in her ears. How did she answer that? She had to go back for the trial. And after that, she planned to resume her old life as a Seattle detective.

Why was she reluctant to be all-in with that plan now? Certainly, she couldn't consider staying here in Lantern Beach. What would she do? It wasn't like the police department was hiring—or that she'd want to work with Bozeman. But those were questions for another day.

"I'm just taking it day by day." Her words caught in her throat, nearly causing her to choke.

"I see." After a moment of silence, Ty cleared his throat. "How's Kujo?"

"Mac is watching him right now. I think he's worried about you."

"Mac or Kujo?"

"Well, probably both. But I was talking about the dog." She squeezed Ty's hand again, noting how it was thick and almost twice as large as hers. Calluses from all the projects he worked on—carpentry and fishing, for starters—roughened his skin. Funny how a person's hands could say so much about a person.

"Would you mind keeping him for a few more days? Or would you ask Mac if he could?"

"Not at all." As Cassidy looked at Ty, an irresistible urge hit her—the urge to reach up and caress his face. To kiss his knuckles. To take care of him.

None of which were things she should do.

Someone knocked at the door. A nurse.

"I need to check vitals," she said. "If you could give us a minute."

Cassidy nodded. "I'll wait outside."

As Cassidy sat in the waiting room once again, she opened the camera on her phone and stared at the pictures of the raft. Just as when she'd seen it the first time in real life, her heart lurched at the shoddy construction of the vessel.

Someone had duct-taped Styrofoam to metal. Covered it all in a tarp with more duct tape. Then they'd trusted that contraption out in open waters, where waves could tower over them and where sharks searched for their next meal.

She turned her head, letting her thoughts run

freely as a realization begged for her attention. Wait . . . was the whole thing made out of a bed frame? It was the right size and shape . . .

Cassidy closed her eyes and imagined being in the Atlantic Ocean, riding out the waves and the storms in one of these. The sun would have been scorching. The waves tumultuous. There was no motor to steer the raft, so the occupants would have to drift, praying they'd make landfall in one piece.

Desperation. Again, the word slammed into her mind. Nobody would get into one of these if they weren't desperate.

Perhaps that was why Cassidy couldn't stop thinking about that raft and its former occupants.

Mac might be right. They might never know what happened to the people who'd constructed the vessel. But that didn't mean Cassidy was going to drop this. Not yet, at least.

"Can I sit here?" someone asked.

"Of course." Cassidy glanced up and saw a young woman, probably in her late teens, standing there, gripping her arm. She looked slightly familiar, but it took a moment to place her. "You work at the Crazy Chefette."

The Crazy Chefette was a restaurant Cassidy's friend Lisa owned.

The woman nodded, her stringy hair falling into her face. "I do. I'm Melissa. I accidentally fell and caught myself on a hot burner in my apartment. I burned the side of my arm."

"I'm sorry to hear that."

"Not as sorry as me. I'm getting together with this guy I've been talking to for the past three months. First time we'll meet face to face. I wanted everything to be perfect."

"A little bandage shouldn't change anything."

She frowned. "I hope not."

"And, if it does, then maybe he's not the guy for you." Oops. Cassidy hadn't meant to offer unsolicited advice. The warning had slipped out before she could stop it.

"You're probably right. I just don't want to lose him. He's . . . well, he's everything I've ever wanted."

"When's he coming into town?"

"Fourth of July. We're going to the parade together."

"I hope you have fun." Cassidy smiled at the stars in the woman's eyes. There was nothing like being in love and all the warm feelings that came with it.

The nurse stepped out of Ty's room, and her eyes connected with Cassidy's. "You're free to go back inside."

"Thank you," she told the nurse before turning to the woman beside her. "Nice meeting you, Melissa. I hope everything goes okay."

Another case of nerves hit Cassidy as she stood. Why was she nervous? Ty was her friend. And that whole admitting he loved her thing? It was just a delirious fluke. The best thing she could do was forget it happened.

Deep inside, Cassidy had to admit that this whole experience had proven her feelings for Ty ran deeper than she realized.

What was she going to do about that? She didn't know.

The important thing right now was that Ty was okay.

He was sitting up in bed looking a little more bright-eyed than when Cassidy stepped inside earlier.

"You don't have to stick around, Cassidy," Ty said, his voice deeper and more gravelly than usual.

"Oh, don't flatter yourself," she teased. "I won't. After all, you were my fake boyfriend for only three days. If I stay here too long, people might start to talk."

His eyes twinkled for the first time since she'd found him on the floor. "We wouldn't want that."

"No, we absolutely wouldn't." She lowered herself in the chair beside him and glanced at his hand, tempted to take it again.

Bad idea. Keep your distance, Cassidy, and remember the end goal: Disbanding DH-7. Don't get distracted.

Ty's phone buzzed on the table. He glanced at the screen and frowned. "It's my mom. Would you mind answering? If she hears my voice, she'll know something is up. Please don't mention this."

Cassidy shrugged. "Sure, but this will cost you one freshly grilled fish dinner once you're feeling better."

"It's a deal."

Cassidy answered. "Hi, Del! How are you feeling?" She honestly wanted to know. She'd been thinking about the woman nonstop.

"I'm hanging in. Just finished my first appointment and I met some of the nicest people at the treatment center."

"I'm glad to hear that."

"How's that son of mine? I thought he was going to call me this morning."

Cassidy glanced at Ty and remembered just why he hadn't called. She hit the speaker button. "He's doing okay. He's right here."

"Hi, Mom," Ty said.

"Tyson, it's good to hear your voice."

"I got distracted this morning. Sorry I didn't check in."

"Oh, that's okay," Del said. "I'm just giving you a hard time. What are you two lovebirds doing?"

They glanced at each other again. Del might kind of, sort of, think the two of them were dating. Long story.

Finally, Ty said, "We're just hanging out."

"Those ordinary moments are the best, aren't they?" Del's warm voice filled the room with her wisdom.

"They really are," Cassidy said. The truth in her words caused a wave of satisfaction to roll over her. That was a lesson she'd been learning more and more lately.

"Okay, I'll let you go," Del said. "Check in later!"

Cassidy felt a smile playing across her lips. Del

made her feel like a part of the family . . . even if she wasn't. Cassidy hadn't even realized how much she loved the feeling of being included, of being a part of a unit. It wasn't something she had back in Seattle. Not really.

Ty studied her a minute. "So, I didn't say anything strange when you found me, did I?"

Cassidy straightened, remembering clearly what he had said. *I love you.* "What do you mean?"

"My mom said when I'm feverish, I spill all my secrets."

"Is that right?" Cassidy asked.

He shrugged. "I just want to make sure I didn't tell you any government secrets."

"Like where terrorists in the Middle East are hiding out? Or what really happened during the Battle of Los Angeles?"

A grin curled his lip. "Yeah, exactly."

"Well—" Before Cassidy could tease him anymore, the door flew open and someone barged into the room.

Cassidy glanced up but didn't recognize the blonde standing there with flowers in her hands. But her eyes were big and bright and set solely on Ty.

Cassidy glanced back at Ty and saw his mouth had dropped open. His gaze fastened on the woman with recognition and disbelief.

"Renee?" Incredulity stretched through his voice.

"Ty?" she squealed. "You won't believe how happy I am to see you!"

Renee? The ex-fiancée who'd dumped Ty before he returned from an overseas deployment? The one who'd given his dog away while he was stationed in the Middle East? The one who'd broken his heart?

What in the world was *she* doing here? And, the even bigger question: why did the woman look so happy?

Chapter Six

TY CHAMBERS' heart pounded into his chest, feeling more like a knife that stabbed him repeatedly. His eyes had to be deceiving him.

Why in the world had Jacqueline Renee Lynch shown up here? He hadn't seen her in three years. Hadn't heard from her. Hadn't so much as received an apology or even a Christmas card.

And now she was in Lantern Beach with her wide grin and happy little gait, acting like nothing had happened between them.

Renee rushed toward his bedside—the opposite of Cassidy—and leaned toward him. The first thing he noticed was the ring on her left hand. The engagement ring that Ty had given her.

She was still wearing it? What. In. The. World?

"It looks like I showed up right on time," Renee purred, her smile bright and overly confident. "What happened, you poor thing?"

He opened his mouth to speak but glanced at Cassidy instead. She stood there with her lips parted and her eyes narrowed. She'd obviously seen the ring also.

Could things get any more awkward? He wanted to explain, but he had no idea what was going on— and that was pretty essential when it came to offering an explanation.

He looked back at Renee, deciding to address her question before focusing on more important matters —matters like why she was wearing that ring. This conversation was like a hot tub—he needed to ease into it.

"It's nothing. Just a little surgery." Ty had put it off until he no longer had a choice—he'd exasperated an old injury from his days as a SEAL.

"Well, it doesn't look like nothing." She thrust the flowers at him. "These are for you."

He took the bouquet and stared at the cheerful yellow daisies, unsure what to do with them. It wasn't every day someone brought him flowers.

Bullets? Yes. Car parts? Definitely. Maybe even his favorite root beer. But never flowers.

"Thank you." He tried to edge off the question at the end of the statement.

Renee's gaze fell on Cassidy, and her smile dimmed. "And who are you? A hospital volunteer?"

Cassidy scowled, the action so slight most people would miss it. But not Ty. He'd spent a lot of time studying those expressions of Cassidy's, trying to memorize them in an effort to figure the woman out. The task seemed futile then and now.

"I'm Cassidy." She paused, her tone no-nonsense. "Ty's neighbor."

"His neighbor? But you weren't the woman I saw there."

"What do you mean?" Cassidy shifted, suspicion in her gaze now.

"Well, I went to your house, Ty, but you didn't answer," Renee explained, her face as perfect as a porcelain doll.

No one could deny she was beautiful. But there were more important things than a person's ability to win a beauty competition. Character truly did count.

"As I walked back down to my car, I ran into this woman next door," Renee continued. "She had a pink ice cream truck and told me you were in the hospital."

Serena, Ty realized. It had to have been Serena.

"I see." His voice sounded dull, even to his own ears. He'd blame his medicine, but he knew there was more to it. "What a surprise."

Cassidy stood and cleared her throat beside them. "You know, I should probably run. Give you guys some time to talk. Maybe lecture Serena about sharing personal information with strangers."

Renee laughed, the sound starting gentle but turning into something that resembled a hyena on speed. Funny how something Ty had once thought cute now sounded worse than Kujo after he stepped on a sand spur.

"You're so funny." Renee ran two manicured fingers through the top of her hair, fluffing it like a pro. "I'm not a stranger. I'm Ty Ty's fiancée."

"You *were* my fiancée," Ty corrected, his heart rate accelerating. Renee being here was *not* good for his health.

Renee looked unaffected by his words as she flung her hand in the air as if she didn't have a care in the world. "We should talk, sweetie."

Sweetie? She had a lot of nerve. But Ty would be a gentleman and hold his tongue. For now.

Cassidy pointed at the door with her thumb. "I'll go. But I'll check on you later, *Ty Ty*."

"Oh, you don't need to do that," Renee said. "I'll take good care of him. I promise. I went to nursing school for three months."

The thing was, Ty didn't want Renee to take care of him. But he did want an explanation as to why she was here.

Cassidy gave him one last look before stepping out the door. It was a look full of questions and amusement. But he couldn't mistake the touch of hurt there also.

And that look was enough to shatter his nerves.

Renee had shown up.

Renee.

Cassidy couldn't stop replaying the encounter at

the clinic.

The fair-weather fiancée had returned. Not only that, but she was wearing an engagement ring. Was it the one Ty had given her? Cassidy had never thought to ask about whether or not she'd given it back. She'd just assumed that Renee had—like any normal woman would.

Cassidy sat in her car outside the clinic and absorbed that information for a minute.

Renee was nothing like Cassidy had envisioned her. In fact, Ty had told Cassidy that his type was the quiet brunette. Renee was neither of those things.

Cassidy's thoughts zoomed ahead in time. What if Ty welcomed Renee back? What if he was gone from Cassidy's life just as quickly as he'd appeared?

She'd like to think it couldn't happen, but she'd seen men act like pigs one too many times. Some men liked their women pretty and shallow. She'd never taken Ty as one of those guys . . . but maybe he was. And maybe it was better if he was. After all, Cassidy had no plans of staying here forever. She had to keep reminding herself of the fact.

Move on, and let Ty live his life. You're just passing through this place, and life with the people here was never supposed to be permanent.

Cassidy's heart ached just a little—no, make that a lot—at the thought. That sentiment was easier in theory than it would be lived out.

She couldn't deny that her heart was unsettled as she went back to her house, ready to get started with her ice cream route. From what everyone had told her, July was the busiest time of year. Cassidy had found it surprisingly fun to talk to vacationers and watch families enjoying each other.

To her surprise, Serena was sitting by the ice cream truck when Cassidy arrived. She fanned her face with what appeared to be a bag and ate a Bomb Pop.

"Serena." Cassidy slammed her car door. "I thought you had a story to cover."

She frowned, pausing from her frantic fanning. "I need your help."

"What's going on?" Cassidy paused and leaned against her car. She had no idea where this was going, but Serena had her full attention. And that meant a lot considering the searing heat and everything that had happened already today.

"I was headed down the street when the tow truck pulled out with the raft on it," Serena said. "Something fell off the back as they were on the highway. No one seemed to notice it. No one but me. So I stopped and picked it up, figuring it was probably nothing. Maybe it was something I could use for a newspaper article."

"That's what you picked up." Cassidy nodded at the bag in her hands.

Serena nodded, raising the object into the air in confirmation. "It is. It was . . . it was more than I anticipated."

"Can I see it?" She stretched out an arm.

Serena handed it to her, an unusual heaviness surrounding her. Whatever was in the bag had shaken her.

Gone was the Serena who tried on different personalities to see what fit. No, this was Serena in her true form. This was Serena scared, shaken, unable to do anything but be herself. It was funny how circumstances could strip people from the airs they tried to put on or the personas they'd been taught to wear. No one knew that better than Cassidy.

Carefully, Cassidy opened the zip-lock bag. Inside, were scraps of paper, it appeared. Actually, it was cardboard and there were two pieces. Three names were scrawled there, each with numbers beneath them.

Social Security numbers, most likely.

Were these the names of the people onboard? If so, these weren't Cuban refugees. No, Cuban refugees wouldn't have Social Security numbers.

Her heart thumped harder as she looked at the next piece.

She realized the cardboard was actually a cereal box that had been ripped apart. And on the back was a message written in what appeared to be lipstick.

If we die, it's the Cobra's fault.

The words felt like a nuclear blast inside her. This was so much bigger than Bozeman had assumed. Whoever had been on this raft were victims.

"Serena, we've got to get this to the police," Cassidy said. "This is much worse than I imagined."

Chapter Seven

"I CAN'T GO to the police." Serena's face grew paler as her eyes reddened. The girl was about to cry.

"Why not?" Cassidy asked, desperately trying to understand the emotions at work here.

She drew in a shaky breath. "What if they arrest me?"

"Just tell them what happened. They have no cause to arrest you."

She shook her head, her motions stiff with fear and panic. She drew her arms across her chest, making it clear she wasn't moving. "I can't."

Cassidy tried not to sound annoyed. "You have to turn this in."

"Please, Cassidy." Her voice quivered.

Cassidy let out a sigh, knowing she needed to choose her battles wisely. *Some battles are not worth fighting. Choose peace instead.*

Another quote from her Day at a Glance, Lucy's

way of speaking to her from the grave, it seemed sometimes. Her friend had always been wise beyond her years.

"You know what?" Cassidy said. "I'll take it in."

"Are you going to mention my name?" Serena's voice cracked as it rose in pitch.

"I'll try not to."

Serena broke from her cocoon of panic, lunged forward, and threw her arms around Cassidy. "Thank you, Cassidy."

"Don't thank me yet." If the police pushed, Cassidy would tell them the truth.

Serena grabbed her car keys from her purse and jangled them in the air. "I've got to get to my interview. You're a lifesaver."

Why did Cassidy have the feeling she'd just been played? Probably because she had.

But that was okay. Because Cassidy wanted some time to examine what Serena had found.

She climbed into Elsa and put the bag in her lap. Carefully, she pulled out the papers inside again, certain not to smudge any potential fingerprints. She took pictures of each with her phone.

Afterward, she went to the police station, as she'd promised.

The chief wasn't in, but Quinton was. Cassidy had met with the officer several times already, and he was pretty consistent with leaking information to her. All it took was a little flattery and girlish charm.

"Well, if it isn't Charity," he said, leaning against

his cluttered desk in the little office he shared with his colleague.

Cassidy scowled but quickly morphed the expression into a flirty one and twirled her blonde hair between her fingers. Every time she employed this tactic, she hated herself for it. Yet, sadly, it usually worked. "It's Cassidy."

"That's right. Cassidy." He nodded like a puppy who'd received a pat on the head. "How could I forget such a pretty name?"

"That's a great question." She kept her voice light and airy, utilizing the acting skills she'd been fine-tuning over the past four months. "Look, I know you guys found that boat earlier. But I think this must have fallen out when you hauled it away."

She handed him the packet, but her fingers took on a mind of their own and refused to let go. Quinton had to pull a little harder than necessary to take the bag from her.

He cast her a strange look, but Cassidy smiled sweetly—as if nothing had happened—and he seemed to forget how odd her iron-clad grip was.

"What is it?" He turned the bag over, acting as if he'd expected a CliffsNotes explanation on the back.

She bit back a smart remark. "I assumed it was trash. But there is a strange little message in it—and some names. Hope it wasn't a bad thing I looked."

"I'm sure you're fine. The raft is pretty much a closed case. Why waste our time when there's no crime? That's what the chief always says."

"Really? Aren't you curious about what happened with that raft?"

"Of course I'm curious. But we have other things to worry about around here."

"I'm sure things are just hopping in Lantern Beach." It killed Cassidy to say the words. The crime on this island was nothing compared to what she'd seen in Seattle. In fact, the murder that occurred when she'd first arrived here was Lantern Beach's first in thirty years.

"You'll look into that, though?" She nodded at the papers. "Just in case. I mean, you seem so thorough."

She gagged again. Being a phony was so hard, especially since she liked to be a straight shooter. This wasn't the way she preferred to live her life.

"Of course." He raised his chin and threw his shoulders back.

Flattery could be infinitely useful.

"Great." Cassidy stepped away but paused. "By the way, where did you guys take the boat?"

"It's behind the station right now. The Coast Guard is coming to inspect it later. Either today or tomorrow."

"I see. How exciting." She just couldn't bring herself to leave, not until she knew this evidence was in good—she'd even take moderately dependable— hands. "By the way, there were some names on those papers."

"Names?" He shuffled the papers until he found them. "My guess is that these are some contacts these refugees had so they could get fake passports and things. We'll double-check."

At least it was *something*. Maybe that was all she could ask for.

―――――

Ty stared at Renee as she bustled around the room, arranging the flowers she'd brought and opening the curtains. She looked so much the same. Still perky. Still blonde. Still the essence of fun and light-heartedness.

Yet there was something missing. What was it? Depth? Stick-to-itiveness? Integrity? Ty wasn't sure, and he might not figure it out until these pain meds wore off some. They'd left him feeling loopy. Not to mention the fact that his shoulder was sore and he didn't want to be here.

"There. Isn't it so much homier now?" Renee turned toward Ty and smiled sweetly.

He wished he could return the action. But he couldn't pretend that the past several years hadn't happened. That Renee hadn't broken his heart and left him when he needed someone the most.

He rubbed his temple, his head pounding. "Renee, what are you doing here?"

Ty hadn't talked to her in forever. She hadn't been interested in talking or explaining or even trying to work things out. And now she showed up and acted as if nothing had happened? That didn't settle right with him.

She sat beside his bed and took his hand, a pleasant—and maybe clueless—smile on her face. "I missed you, Ty."

"It took you three years to realize that?"

She let out a lighthearted sigh and stared into the distance. "I know it might sound crazy, but I just had this realization. It literally struck me like a lightning bolt. I finally recognized what we had, and how much I missed you, and I couldn't imagine my future without my Ty Ty."

He cringed at the pet name—he'd never liked it, but especially not now. "What caused this realization?"

It wasn't that simple. It never was with Renee. At one time, Ty had wanted to believe whatever she told him. It was almost like the woman had cast a spell on him. And that was the most dangerous kind of infatuation, mostly because it wasn't grounded in reality or truth. But not anymore. He'd learned that lesson the hard way.

"It was really just an accumulation of things." She offered no more information, just a slight shrug. But Ty would bet her "realization" had something to do with another man and a freshly ended relationship.

"You left me, Renee," he reminded her, keeping his voice placid. He didn't want to stir up any emotions by getting irritated or angry or impatient.

No, he'd remain even-keeled for as long as possible—all for the sake of civility.

Turn the other cheek. He'd read it in his Bible a couple of days ago, along with other verses about forgiveness and living out love.

Renee leaned closer and lowered her voice. "And now I want to make things right."

A flash of irritation shot down his spine. She was greatly simplifying this situation. "Sometimes you can't make things right. Sometimes you make choices and have to live with the consequences."

Her bottom lip jutted out in a pout that would have, at one time, twisted his resolve and tugged at his heartstrings. Not anymore. "What's life without second chances?"

"Renee . . ." Had she heard a word Ty had said?

"Steve told me you were all about second chances. Said you'd become a new man since you got out of the military."

"Steve? When did you talk to Steve?" Steve was the mutual friend who'd introduced them. He'd been stationed back in San Diego before their breakup, but Ty talked to him every once in a while.

"Last week. How do you think I knew where you were? No way I could have tracked you to the middle of nowhere on my own."

Ty was going to have to have a long talk with his friend. He decided to try a different approach to this conversation. "This is all very sudden and abrupt. I had no idea you were going to show up."

Renee squeezed his hand tighter and peered at him with her big, doe-like eyes. "I know. Isn't it great?"

"Renee—"

"Look, I'm here, and my plane doesn't leave for three days. Can't we talk and make amends? I don't know what that will look like or what that means. I just know that I hate the way things ended. I want to be a new woman as well."

She had to be kidding. "The way things *ended*? You mean the way *you left things*?"

Her pout grew larger. "Please, Ty. It sounds so harsh when you put it like that."

Ty's gut twisted. He started to tell her she needed to go, but before he could, Renee jumped to her feet.

"You won't regret this, Ty. And this is perfect timing because you need someone in your corner right now, and here I am." She leaned down and kissed his cheek. "I can even sleep on that little couch here in your room while you're at the clinic. I brought a blanket and everything."

"You don't have to do that," Ty said, exhausted at the mere thought.

"Oh, I insist." She glanced at the door. "In fact, let me run and get some snacks for us. I'm going to need to eat while I'm here. You still like kettle corn?"

"No, I've never liked—"

But, before Ty could finish, Renee was gone.

He released a long breath and pushed his head back into the pillow behind him.

How in the world had this even happened?

The whole encounter made him realize how much he'd changed over the past few years. He wasn't the man he used to be, and he actually liked the new person he'd become. When he'd been engaged to Renee, he'd been preoccupied a majority of the time with his job. When he'd returned home from his various deployments, he may have left the battlefield behind physically, but mentally he'd remained in Iraq.

He hadn't even realized it back then, but now those facts were as clear as day. He'd lived and breathed being a Navy SEAL. And then it was all gone—and so was Renee.

Besides, the heartache and trials he'd been through—and he'd had plenty—had led him back to his faith. Led him back to what was important in life.

So all of it wasn't bad.

But he had no intention of rekindling a romance with Renee. He just needed to make that clear to her. However, that wasn't as easy as it sounded.

Chapter Eight

AS PER HER NORMAL WORKDAY, Cassidy drove up and down the streets of Lantern Beach selling ice cream. She'd developed her pattern, one that allowed her to hit every road in town.

She wanted to skip it all today and rush home to her computer to look up those names from the package Serena had found. But reality was that if Cassidy didn't make some money, she wasn't going to be able to buy any groceries. So she needed to put in her time making her rounds before she dug further into this mystery.

If she was smart, she wouldn't dig into it at *all*. But . . .

As she drove past the clinic, her thoughts drifted to Ty. How was he? Was Renee taking good care of him?

Cassidy's stomach squeezed at the thought. Which was stupid. She and Ty were just friends, and nothing else. If he wanted to get back together with the woman who'd broken his heart then that was his right.

Yet, despite that, her thoughts felt like they were stampeding out ahead of her and she couldn't catch up to gain control.

Had Ty called Renee? Asked her to come? Had they been talking before this?

The thoughts bothered Cassidy, even though they shouldn't. Ty wasn't hers, yet somewhere down the line she'd begun to believe the lie that he was. A seed of hope had been planted that maybe—just maybe—they could have a future together. But Cassidy knew good and well that was an unlikely scenario.

She pushed aside her feelings—they would get her nowhere. Instead, she headed down more streets. As she reached the road before her house, she slowed.

Interesting. A Lexus was parked at one of the small bungalows.

She might not have noticed it except for the fact that expensive cars like that usually showed up at expensive houses right on the water. The car and the primitive-looking rental didn't belong together.

She also passed a house with kids running back and forth through sprinklers. They squealed with delight, the sound of their laughter making Cassidy warm inside. So much of her career recently had left her feeling cynical and jaded. The simple acts of kids being kids and enjoying themselves made her work here more pleasurable than she could have imagined.

The house at the end of the lane made her pause every time she passed. The place was probably a much-loved cottage at one time, but now it sat in the midst of largely overgrown brush and seagrass. She could hardly see the house because the shrubs and trees had grown so much. But it was there, hidden by nature.

Something looked different about it today. She hit the brakes and stared at the place a minute.

On the outside, there was nothing visible to hint at what nagged at her. All the shrubs were still in place. Had some of the grass been disturbed?

Maybe that was it.

It was probably nothing. Maybe some kids had gone to retrieve a wayward ball or something.

Your mind always goes to the worst places, Cassidy.

There were probably twenty or thirty homes on the island that hadn't received visitors—or owners—in years. Maybe they'd been handed down from generation to generation. Maybe the owners' lives had changed and they were no longer able to come. Who knew what their stories were.

Still, this one had her attention for some reason.

"Can I buy some ice cream?"

The sound of someone's sweet little voice on the other side of the vehicle nearly made Cassidy jump out of her seat.

She turned to see a little girl standing there, her hand outstretched with a dollar bill.

"It's the perfect treat after playing in the sprinkler," the girl's mom said, running up behind her wearing a bikini top barely covering her fit body.

"I think I need to get some sprinklers like that." Cassidy smiled. "They look super fun."

"Even better, they're motion-activated," the mom said. "And please tell me you have Choco Tacos?"

"As a matter of fact I do." Cassidy shoved her earlier thoughts aside and plastered on a smile as she scooted to the back of the truck. "What else can I get for you?"

Three hours later, Cassidy pulled up to the Crazy Chefette. Her friend Lisa Garth used her background in science to create fabulous food experiments. In truth, her combinations were genius. Especially her grilled-cheese-and-peach sandwich.

Cassidy stepped inside and glanced around. To her surprise, Mac wasn't there entertaining anyone who would listen with his stories or with his talent for saying the alphabet backwards and skipping every other letter.

Cassidy did spot Serena, Skye, and Austin at a corner table. They waved her over, and Cassidy slid in beside Serena.

"Did you turn it in?" Serena whispered.

"I did. No problems." Cassidy grabbed a paper menu with today's specials. "How was your interview?"

"In truth, it was a little boring." Serena frowned. "But I'm determined to think of a way to make it interesting."

"It was with the parade organizer, right?" Cassidy asked.

Serena nodded. "Yeah, but he doesn't have great PR skills, and he mostly wanted to talk about the boat that washed ashore."

"Is that right?" Cassidy said. She could see where the boat would be interesting.

"Niles isn't the most personable guy," Austin said. "I did some work on his house. He only likes the finest things in life, which is strange considering he lives here. Lantern Beach is a place for people who want to get away from it all, not for people looking for a slice of the fancy life."

"Well, what does he do full-time?" Cassidy asked.

"I think he's the city manager," Serena said. "He does something with the local government. I guess I should have asked him more about that during the interview."

"Well, I'm sure you'll think of a way to make the story interesting."

"I did hear that Martin Chaser is going to be the Grand Marshal," Serena said. "That's interesting."

"Who's Martin Chaser?" The name sounded vaguely familiar.

"He's a racecar driver out of Charlotte," Austin said. "He's not the best out there, but he's pretty good."

The waitress came to take their orders. Cassidy recognized her from the clinic. Melissa, if she remembered correctly.

"Hey, I know you," Cassidy said. "How's your arm?"

Melissa turned sideways and showed Cassidy her bandage. "A little medicine and it will be all better. Could have been worse."

"Glad to hear you're okay."

"Me too. Now what can I get you?"

Cassidy ordered the Burger with Butter—a hamburger topped with peanut butter. It normally wouldn't be her first choice, but Lisa hadn't let Cassidy down yet with her crazy combinations. The rest of the gang also ordered an assortment of food—fish tacos, crab-cake sandwiches, and hamburgers.

"By the way, how's Ty doing?" Austin asked.

Cassidy frowned when she remembered the events from earlier today. "He's doing okay, especially now that his fiancée is here to take care of him."

Skye's mouth dropped open. "His fiancée?"

"Well, his ex-fiancée. But she didn't look very *ex*y to me. She was even wearing an engagement ring." Cassidy had never been much of a gossip, but she felt like one now. She'd be wise to watch what she said.

Gossip dies when it hits a wise person's ears.

Be wise, Cassidy. Be wise.

"That is very interesting," Skye said.

"Isn't it, though?" Cassidy needed to stop talking. She hadn't intended on sharing that much, yet the thoughts had been dancing around in her head since Renee had shown up. "Who's that man over there?"

Cassidy nodded toward a man wearing a business suit in the distance. She might not have noticed him, but a gaggle of people had gathered around. Were they asking for autographs?

"Smith Anderson," Austin said. "He's a news anchor for a station out of Raleigh."

"Is he here to cover the parade?" Cassidy asked.

He wasn't dressed like a vacationer. No, he looked all business.

"I heard he was buying a house," Austin said.

"Happy house hunting," Skye said.

Lisa appeared just then. As usual, her lab coat—used in lieu of an apron—was splattered with evidence of her latest recipe inventions. "If it's not my favorite group of people. Except for Will. Where is Will?"

"He's keeping busy with people's pool pumps breaking down and hot tubs getting clogged," Austin said. "Not to mention the sunset kayaking tours."

"So busy he can't stop by and see us?" Lisa swung the paper bag in her hands.

"I'll fuss at him next time I see him," Skye said.

"You do that. I see you met Melissa."

"I did. She must be one of your newer employees," Cassidy said.

Lisa nodded. "Just came to town from somewhere up north. Kind of quiet, but I have hopes she'll find her place here. She just seems kind of lonely, you know? And accident prone." Lisa turned to Cassidy. "Anyway, I don't know where that came from. Cassidy, could you give these to Ty? It's a new recipe I just came up with."

"Oh, yeah? What is it?" Cassidy asked.

"Salt-and-vinegar sugar cookies."

Cassidy's stomach turned at the thought.

"I know what you're thinking," Lisa said. "But they're good. I promise. They're sugar cookies mixed with an entire extra-large bag of salt-and-vinegar chips that have been crumbled. It has this great sweet and salty vibe going. Besides, have I ever let you down before?"

"No . . ." Cassidy sounded uncertain.

"Will you take them to him?"

Cassidy hesitated, desperately trying to come up with an excuse and a reason to put distance between herself and Ty. "I'm just not sure I'm going to have time today. I have a full schedule . . . selling ice cream."

Everyone stared at her, and she knew not one of them bought it.

Finally, she released her breath. "Of course, I'll drop them off for him."

Lisa smiled. "Thanks. I gotta go!"

Cassidy stared at the bag of cookies. She wasn't sure what she dreaded more. Seeing Ty and Renee. Or knowing she was going to have to try one of these.

Cassidy fanned herself with her hands against the heat outside. The sun's rays seemed to reflect from every visible surface around her, causing solar waves to thicken the air.

This was one of the few things that made her miss Seattle. The humidity here made everything feel ten times hotter.

She paced to Elsa at the far end of the lot. It had been crowded when Cassidy arrived, so she'd parked partially on the grass and nearly blocked the dumpster. Thankfully, she knew today wasn't trash day at the restaurant, so it would be okay.

As she started to open her door, a voice in the distance caused her pause.

It sounded like a man. But where was he?

She leaned forward and noticed someone had ducked behind the restaurant.

That was Smith Anderson, she realized.

She drew back before he spotted her, wondering what exactly he was doing behind the building. A moment later, his words drifted out to her.

"I don't want anyone in town to know about this," he grumbled. "It will cause my likability factor to plummet. The last thing I need is to give people time to start a petition or something."

What in the world . . .

"Well, they'll get used to it," he continued. "Life goes on, and no one can control everything that goes on around them. You just have to learn to live with it."

There was a pause in the conversation. He was obviously talking on the phone, and the other person was responding to him now.

Cassidy would love to hear what the person on the other end was saying.

"You need to make this deal happen." Smith's voice rose. "You need to convince the powers that be that this move would be great for Lantern Beach. Not everyone who comes here wants to rent a house or stay in that dinky little inn. The island needs to change with the times."

What exactly was he planning? The tone of his voice made it clear that he not only felt passionate, but that he was also angry. Maybe controlling. Power hungry.

All those things raised warning flags in her mind.

Smith Anderson hadn't come here to buy himself a house.

"I'm building that hotel if it's the last thing I do!"

Yep, he wanted to build something bigger.

As footsteps stormed her way, Cassidy ducked behind her ice cream truck. She peered out in time to see his stiff gait, his red cheeks.

He was someone to keep an eye on. Did he have anything to do with this mystery? Maybe. Maybe not.

Only time would tell.

Chapter Nine

CASSIDY PAUSED outside Ty's door at the clinic and raised her hand to knock. Before she could, the door flew open.

Renee stood there.

The woman's eyes brightened when she saw Cassidy. "You were here earlier. The volunteer, right?"

"I'm Ty's neighbor," Cassidy reminded her. If the woman had forgotten that quickly, she really did have issues. Maybe she'd had a memory lapse, and that was why she thought she was still engaged.

"You're the one who found him?" She stepped outside and closed the door behind her. "I guess I owe you a thanks."

Cassidy shrugged, unsure what to say. She hadn't helped Ty because of Renee, but Cassidy wasn't going to quibble over something that minor. "It wasn't a problem."

"If something had happened to him, then he and

I would never have a chance to try again. So it is a big deal—a big deal to me." Something that tried a little too hard to sound like sincerity dripped from her voice.

Then Renee's words hit her.

"Trying again?" Cassidy repeated, certain she hadn't heard correctly.

Then again, maybe Cassidy was the one confused here. She'd thought she knew Ty. She thought he'd made his feelings for her clear. But maybe deep inside this whole time, he still cared about Renee. Maybe they had been talking. Maybe he *wanted* Renee to show up here.

Maybe he was one of *those* guys.

Her heart ached a little at the thought.

"Things didn't end well between us. It's a shame when something beautiful ends on an ugly note. Ty has always loved me. And he always will. That's what he said." Renee's words were pointed, as if she wanted to get her message across loud and clear.

The blood drained from Cassidy's face. "He told you that?"

Renee giggled. "Isn't he great? He's a real man, not the kind who likes to give up on people or relationships. He told me how important forgiveness is, as well as second chances."

That last part sounded like him. Ty had made plenty of mistakes, but he had a good heart and always wanted to do the honorable thing. Did he consider it honorable to fulfill his previous commitment to Renee? It didn't make sense to Cassidy, but maybe he viewed his engagement as a commitment that hadn't ended.

Cassidy cleared her throat. "So you'll be sticking around here?"

"Oh, no. Not if I have anything to do with it. I think we should start over somewhere new. Maybe New York City. Probably somewhere smaller, though. Atlanta? LA would be totally out of the question."

Cassidy almost couldn't stomach the thought of Ty leaving. Which was ridiculous. Because Cassidy had to leave one day.

She hated it when her emotions got the best of her. And that's exactly what they were doing right now. They were volleying back and forth, back and forth, between logic and emotion, between reality and desire.

"You've talked to Ty about this?" Cassidy finally asked, shifting her weight from one leg to the other as she tried to figure out how to proceed.

"Oh, we've been talking and talking. It's been great. It's almost like we were never apart."

Suddenly, Cassidy's confusion turned into anger. Protectiveness. Justice. At the moment, it didn't matter what he'd decided. If Ty truly did or didn't want to get back together with Renee. What mattered right now was that Renee had deeply hurt Ty. Cassidy didn't want to see that happen again.

She stepped closer, and Renee's smile dimmed.

"You may fool other people with your Little Miss Innocent Act, but not me."

"You've got me all wrong." Renee's gaze sliced through her. She obviously did not appreciate being questioned.

"Oh, I doubt that. How you left Ty was deplorable. If you hurt him again, then I suggest you never show your face around me or you will regret it."

Renee gasped and stepped back. "Regret it how?"

Cassidy recalled the stash of guns that she had. The training she'd been through. Of course, she would never employ those things on Renee, however tempted she might be.

Instead, she said, "I might use some information I've learned here as a hospital volunteer to make your life miserable."

"I thought you said you were his neighbor."

Cassidy let out a cynical laugh. "I'm not even going to acknowledge that. But I will end with this. People with integrity don't run away so they don't have to face the consequences of their actions."

"That's so insulting."

She thrust the paper bag into Renee's hands. "And here are some cookies for Ty."

She turned and walked away before she said anything more she'd regret.

"Are you in love with him?" Renee called.

Cassidy? In love? The thought was ridiculous.

So ridiculous that she didn't bother to acknowledge the remark, nor did she admit to herself that her heart felt a little broken.

"Who was that?" Ty asked, eyeing Renee suspiciously.

"Oh, just the volunteer from the clinic. I mean, your neighbor. Yeah, that's right. Your neighbor. She dropped these by." Renee handed him a paper bag, but she didn't look nearly as perky as she had earlier.

He glanced inside and saw some cookies there.

"My neighbor?" Ty said. Cassidy had been here? "She didn't stay?"

He'd been hoping he would have a chance to see Cassidy and catch up. What exactly had Renee told her? His stomach churned at the thought.

"She said she had stuff to do at home and couldn't stay." Renee plopped back down beside him and filed her nails.

Couldn't stay? Disappointment bit into him.

He desperately wanted time alone. Or time with Cassidy. But no more with Renee. The woman was on his last nerve, and she wouldn't take a hint. Or even a direct statement, for that matter.

"On a separate note, there was some scary-looking guy out there," Renee said.

"Scary how?"

"I don't know. He has this huge tattoo on his bicep of some type of snake. What kind of people hang out on this island?"

"Interesting." She seemed to be changing the subject for some reason.

"Okay, well, I'm just going to go ahead and turn in for the night. I'm bushed after the flight and renting a car and coming here to find you like this." She grabbed a blanket embellished with oversized pink and red hearts.

"You really don't have to stay," Ty said.

He didn't want to stay either. He couldn't stand the smell of the clinic. Was already tired of the food. He missed Kujo.

"Oh, you couldn't pry me away with a crowbar." Renee smiled.

That was what he was afraid of.

"Do you care if I watch *The Bachelor*? It should be on in reruns," Renee said, grabbing the remote.

He couldn't think of anything he wanted to watch less. But if Renee watched her show, she might stop talking for a while and give him time to gather his thoughts.

He picked up his phone from beside his bed and considered calling or texting Cassidy.

But explaining this situation needed more than a phone call or text message.

He let out a sigh and leaned back.

Tomorrow, he decided. Tomorrow he would make things right. First, he needed to get a little more of his energy back because it was going to take a lot out of him to get through to Renee.

Once back at her house, Cassidy sat down at her computer. The sun had set, and darkness had descended on the island. The cottage felt surprisingly lonely, and she had no idea why. She was always here by herself.

But, tonight, Ty was at the clinic and Kujo was at Mac's for the night.

Apparently, the dog was doing great in his training and was officially deemed an expert cheese finder. The thought made Cassidy smile.

But her grin faded as she thought about her conversation with Renee.

Had Ty really told the woman he still loved her? That he wanted another chance?

Though Cassidy had already tried to sort through the thoughts and questions, they came back again. Ty was the honorable type of guy—maybe he wanted to see their relationship to completion. Or maybe this wasn't about honor—maybe he still loved the woman. Renee was beautiful and perky. Maybe he hadn't gotten over her.

Ultimately, those tumultuous thoughts were the real reason Cassidy felt so alone right now. And that wasn't okay. Her heart was never supposed to get involved in all this.

She came here with a mission, and she'd somehow lost her focus. However, she couldn't deny that her temporary life here seemed so much more fulfilling than what she'd left behind. She was going to have to grapple with those realizations sometime in the future. But now wasn't the time.

Cassidy sighed. She really needed to concentrate on something else.

She pulled out her phone, and found the photos she'd taken of those papers Serena had found. She typed the first name into her search bar. Kat Bolton.

Cassidy squinted at the results. Though the name didn't seem that common, a surprising number of people had that moniker. She scrolled through the first ten but didn't find any information that seemed to link the name to the raft that had washed up.

She typed in the next name. Trina Smith. Cassidy didn't have much hope for better luck with this search.

And, as suspected, she didn't find any good leads.

The third name was Rose Alvarez. Cassidy scrolled through the results, stopping at one article.

Rose Alvarez. Age nineteen. Arrested for sale and distribution of drugs in Charleston, South Carolina.

The woman in the mug shot had dark hair and tan skin that indicated a possible Latino heritage.

Could she be the same person whose name was on this paper? Perhaps the woman had gotten involved with something illegal, like the chief had suggested. Were these names a list of contacts that the occupants of that raft were supposed to make once they hit land?

Cassidy shook her head. She didn't know.

Yet she couldn't stop thinking about the boat.

Couldn't stop ruminating on the questions in her mind. Perhaps thinking about someone else's problems was more intriguing than remembering her own. Or maybe it was because selling ice cream wasn't her calling.

Her cell phone rang. Her secret one.

She retrieved it and saw that it was Samuel. She quickly put the phone to her ear. "Twice in one day? What's the occasion?"

"Cassidy, your parents contacted me today after we talked," he said.

They'd finally noticed she was missing, huh? Perhaps the excuse that was going around—that Cassidy had taken an extended vacation—didn't ring quite true to them. It had only taken six weeks.

"Okay . . ." She braced herself for what he might say.

"They're very concerned about you, and they've hired a private investigator to find out more information."

Her lungs tightened. "They did what?"

Her parents had more money than they knew what to do with. That meant they'd hire the best in the business. They'd give him cash to fly where he needed and to do whatever necessary to track her down.

"You heard me."

She'd almost told her parents that she was going into hiding. But her absence wouldn't disrupt their lives—she was surprised they'd even noticed. Instead, she'd told friends and colleagues she was taking a sabbatical. The fewer people who knew what she was really doing, the better.

"Do you know who the PI is?" Cassidy asked, trying to flesh out the situation in her mind.

"Ricky Ernest."

"Ricky Ernest?" Cassidy couldn't believe it. She'd dated Ricky one summer during college. Why in the world would her parents hire him?

Calm down, Cassidy. Just because they hired him doesn't mean he'll find you.

"Be careful," Samuel warned. "I'd hate for this guy to ruin our plans."

"Yeah, so would I. Maybe you should tell my parents to call him off. Tell them I'm out of town working a case or something."

"I don't want anyone to link me with your disappearance," Samuel said. "It's too risky. Don't worry—we've covered our bases. This guy shouldn't find you."

Cassidy hung up, but she didn't feel nearly as certain as Samuel.

Cassidy had decided to sleep on the couch that evening, hoping she'd be more alert and wake quickly if anything happened during the night. Namely if someone decided to raid her ice cream truck again.

Her bet paid off. At 2:30 a.m., a noise sounded

downstairs. It was ever-so-slight. Whispers. Soft footsteps.

The sounds were so faint, Cassidy wondered if she'd imagined them. But she hadn't. The whines and taps were real.

Cassidy grabbed a gun from a compartment hidden in a kitchen drawer. She tucked it into her waistband and slowly—quietly—crept outside. She paced softly down the steps. Just before the bottom, she paused and crouched.

Someone was definitely in her truck, stealing her inventory.

Though Cassidy wanted to pounce, an internal voice told her to wait.

So she did.

It was too dark to see what was going on or how many people were here. Part of her suspected some of the local kids were up to mischief. Another part of her hoped for more—hoped for a connection with that raft.

Maybe it was just wishful thinking, though.

Finally, the scurrying inside her truck stopped, and two figures emerged.

Through the darkness, Cassidy thought they were women, but she couldn't be certain.

The thieves started to depart from Cassidy's place, moving toward the small stretch of woods between her street and the next row of beach houses.

Cassidy decided to follow.

Keeping her pace measured, she stayed behind them, careful to remain in the shadows.

As she reached the woods, she wished she'd taken time to pull on some shoes. But she hadn't so she needed to contend with that. She only hoped she didn't step on any snakes or sandspurs.

Though the maritime forest here was only a thin sliver, it was still thick with scrubby little plants and short, bushy trees. Based on the tracks Cassidy saw in the sand near her house, raccoons and maybe some fox called this place home, not to mention the biting flies, mosquitoes, and ticks.

As she dodged a low-lying live oak tree, a branch snapped beneath her feet.

The women in front of her paused.

Cassidy slipped behind the trunk, scolding herself for not seeing the branch. Well, she *had* seen it, but she'd thought it was a root.

The women whispered before taking off in a run.

Cassidy carefully stayed behind them, desperate not to lose them.

She stopped at the abandoned house she'd noticed on her ice cream route earlier this afternoon.

Those women were staying here, she realized. That's why something had looked different. Because it had been. The grass had been trampled by the house's new—and perhaps uninvited—residents.

Cassidy froze, trying to formulate her next plan of action. She didn't want to spook them. But something told her these women needed her help.

Carefully she wandered through the thick underbrush until she stood at the base of the stairway leading to the front door. She stared up, beyond the rickety boards in front of her. There was no easy or good way to do this. Whoever was inside was frightened. Would be on edge. Might even be ready to attack.

But Cassidy couldn't turn back now.

Quietly, she climbed until she reached the second story deck. She pressed herself against the exterior wall and peered through a window. It was no use. Blinds and curtains covered the glass.

As she looked down, something at her feet caught her eye. She squatted down, touched a pool of liquid there, and put her fingers to her nose. A metallic scent filled her nostrils.

Blood.

Once you smelled it, the odor became unmistakable.

Someone inside this house was injured.

Cassidy had to do something.

Swallowing hard, she gripped the door handle. To her surprise, it turned. With a touch of hesitation, she pushed it open.

She sucked in a deep breath at the scene on the other side.

Three women sat in the living room, all huddled around a hurricane lantern that spilled light around it.

All their attention turned to Cassidy, their fear so palpable it crackled the air.

"I'm not going to hurt you." Cassidy raised her hands. "I want to help."

One of the women grabbed a knife from the table beside her and thrashed toward Cassidy—fear and vengeance in her wild eyes. Sweat covered the woman's forehead and cheeks—sweat due to terror. Or maybe because there was no AC in the house and the windows were locked tight. The inside was sweltering.

"Stay back," the woman warned, wielding the knife.

Cassidy recognized her. It was Rose Alvarez. These were the women from the raft.

They weren't refugees. No, they were victims. She just wasn't sure what they were victims of.

"You should put that knife down," Cassidy urged. "I'm not going to cause trouble."

Rose stepped closer, that crazy look still in her eyes. "You're right. You're not going to cause any trouble. I'm going to make sure of that."

Cassidy stared at the blade, wondering what exactly she'd gotten herself into.

Chapter Ten

CASSIDY RAISED her hands higher while sinking her voice lower. "I want to help."

"Who are you?" Rose demanded, swatting at a bug.

That was when Cassidy realized just how primitive the conditions were inside this place. Not only was it hot, but it smelled like sewage. There was a hole in the roof at the corner of the room. Mosquitoes were everywhere, and Cassidy suspected the movement on the kitchen counter had been a cockroach.

She swallowed hard, glancing at Rose's knife again. "I'm the woman who owns the ice cream truck you keep stealing food from."

Rose frowned. "We'll pay you back."

Cassidy nodded to the woman on the couch. "Your friend needs help."

"We'll handle it."

Cassidy's gaze focused for a moment on the injured woman. She had red hair that was short and curly, and her mop-like style only emphasized her round face. But it was her pinched expression and the cloth tied around her foot that caught Cassidy's attention.

"Your friend on the couch is hurt," she said. "She needs to see a doctor."

"No doctors!" Rose's voice climbed with emotion. "You just need to mind your own business. You should have never come here. And how could you have forgotten to lock the door, Trina?"

The other woman shook her head and backed up slightly. She was the mousy, frail, and entirely too thin one of the group. Her stringy brown hair looked like it hadn't been washed in days, and her motions were jerky and fearful.

"I'm sorry," Trina said.

"I wish you hadn't come here," Rose said. "Because I don't know that we're going to be able to let you leave."

A chill ran down Cassidy's spine. "Don't be ridiculous. I only want to help."

"We didn't ask for no help!" Rose stared at her, nostrils flaring.

Cassidy remembered the gun at her waistband—how could she forget it?—but she'd use it only in an emergency. As soon as she pulled it out, mayhem would scatter its chaos. The emotions in the room were already high enough.

"Well, when you stole from me, you got me involved," Cassidy said, using her best negotiator voice. Yet her muscles were poised to fight if that's what it came down to.

"You need to leave us alone."

Cassidy palmed her hands in the air. "Can I check on your friend?"

"Are you a paramedic?"

"No, but I've taken first aid classes."

Rose stared, her eyes hard. "Fine. Check on her. But I'm watching you."

Cassidy moved past Rose slowly, not willing to take a chance Rose would do anything rash. When she reached the woman on the couch, she knelt beside her. Cassidy carefully pulled back the cloth from around the injured foot. A large gash sliced the bottom.

Was this where the bloody cloth on the raft had come from?

"How long has she been like this?" Cassidy asked.

"Two days," Trina said. "She cut her foot on some metal while we were . . . while we were out."

On the raft. Cassidy silently filled in the missing details.

"Have you given her anything?" Cassidy asked.

"We don't have anything to give her," Rose spat. "We're just trying to make her comfortable."

"Let me go back to my place and get some medicine. Maybe a first aid kit so you can bandage the wound."

Trina didn't respond, only looked at Rose, who was obviously the ringleader of this bunch.

Rose didn't say anything for a minute. Finally, she nodded. "Okay. But I'm going with you."

"You don't have to do that." Cassidy preferred to go alone instead of with a crazy woman with a knife.

"How do I know you won't call the police when you leave here?"

Cassidy met her gaze. "How do you know I will?"

Rose narrowed her eyes. "I'm not in the mood to play games."

"I'm not trying to play games." Cassidy kept her voice even. "Look, you don't know me. I understand that you're not sure if I'm trustworthy. But I'm not going to call the police."

"We stole your food," she reminded.

"I don't endorse stealing, but it's obvious you're all hungry. I'm not concerned about that right now. All I'm concerned about is this woman. Since you won't take her to a doctor, I need to do what I can to help."

"I'm still going with you," Rose said. "I need to make sure you stick to your word."

Cassidy didn't have time to argue. "Fine. Come with me. But I wish you'd put that knife away."

"This is just insurance in case you do something stupid."

Cassidy finally nodded, hoping she wouldn't have to do things the hard way. "Okay then. Let's go."

Cassidy couldn't forget about the blade Rose held against her back as if she was leading a criminal to execution. One wrong move, and Rose could seriously injure—or kill—Cassidy.

That was why it was so important for everyone to keep a level head. And for Cassidy and Rose to watch their steps on the uneven, sandy ground.

She wound her way through the trees, heading back to her cottage. The darkness out here was blinding and much darker than that Cassidy had experienced back in Seattle. On Lantern Beach, there weren't even streetlights. No, this darkness was authentic and unbridled.

Despite her mental warning to watch her steps, Cassidy's foot caught on something—another root, this one concealed by either sand or darkness or both. She started to fall forward but caught herself before she hit the ground.

"You've got a gun," Rose hissed behind her.

Cassidy's shirt must have come up and revealed her weapon. Her stomach sank. She knew how this would look to someone already on edge.

"I do." There was no use denying it.

Rose stepped closer, leering at Cassidy with pure defiance and undeniable menace. "Who are you?"

"I told you. I sell ice cream."

"Then why do you have a gun?"

"Because I'm a single lady. You can never be too safe. If you haven't noticed, I didn't pull it out, and I've had plenty of opportunities."

Rose held her hand out. "Give it to me."

Cassidy raised her chin. "No."

"You do realize I have a knife, don't you?"

"And you do realize I have a gun, don't you?"

The two women stared off at each other, pacing in a circle like two fighters in center ring.

"I don't trust you," Rose finally barked.

"It doesn't look like you have much choice but to try and trust me right now," Cassidy said. "You don't appear to have anyone else in your corner."

"You should have never gotten involved in this, lady."

"I'm beginning to see that. But I'm involved now, whether I want to be or not."

"Keep moving," Rose ordered. "And if I see you reaching for that gun, I won't hesitate to use this knife. I've got a black belt in tae-kwarving-o."

She was tough and funny.

Cassidy didn't mention that she could draw her gun and shoot in three seconds flat. Instead, she acted compliant and kept moving. Questions danced at the edge of her tongue, but she didn't ask them. This wasn't the time. No, she needed to develop some trust with the woman first.

They reached her house, and Cassidy opened the door.

"I'm going to go get the first aid kit," Cassidy said. "You can watch me."

"Don't worry. I will." Rose stationed herself at the door, her eyes still cold and street-wise. Or was it street-hardened?

Cassidy didn't know the woman's story and didn't have time to piece everything together yet. No, right now, it was all about survival—for her and for these ladies.

She grabbed the kit from the kitchen—she'd stashed one beneath the sink. She slipped it into a paper sack from the grocery store and paused. "You all need more food."

Rose didn't say anything.

"I don't have much. It's time for me to go shopping again. But I'm going to grab what I have. Okay?"

Rose nodded.

Cassidy reached into her fridge and pulled out some bread. Some lunch meat and cheese. From her pantry, she got some soup and crackers and granola bars. It wasn't much, but these were all things they could eat without electricity—Cassidy was pretty sure there wasn't any at the house where they were staying.

"What else do you need?" Cassidy asked. "Clothes? Blankets?"

"We don't need nothing else."

She sighed, this struggle getting old. "I'm not

trying to impose, but obviously you all need things. You're staying in an abandoned house and stealing food from my ice cream truck."

Rose's nostrils flared again as she stood there stiffly. "Fine. Some clothes would be nice. Maybe some soap and a towel or two."

"I have to go down the hallway."

"I'll go with you."

"I'd expect nothing less."

"Don't be smart."

"I'm being honest." Cassidy walked down the hallway, keenly aware that the situation could turn ugly in the blink of an eye.

She slipped into her room and began gathering some extra clothing from her dresser.

"You don't live here full time," Rose said, glancing around the room. "This looks like a rental. There's nothing personal."

"I'm only here for the summer."

"Where you from?"

"Texas," Cassidy glanced up. "How about ya'll?"

"It's not important."

She stuffed the last of the clothes into a duffel bag and then went to the bathroom and gathered some toiletries. "Will that work?"

"It's great."

"Let's go then. Your friend needs that medicine ASAP." She heaved the bag onto her back and grabbed the paper bag from the kitchen.

Her hands were full, which didn't bode well in

case she needed to draw her weapon. She was going to have to cross that bridge when she got there.

"Why do you want to help us?" Rose asked as they started down the steps.

"Isn't that what you're supposed to do if you see someone in need?"

"Most people would say no."

"Then you haven't met the right kind of people."

"I guess I haven't." Rose moved beside her—a sign she was starting to trust her—but she still held that outstretched knife. "Most people want something in exchange for doing something nice for you."

"I'm not asking for anything in return." Cassidy almost added "Rose," but remembered she wasn't supposed to know the woman's name.

Thank goodness she'd stopped herself from saying it because things could have turned ugly otherwise.

"Stop," Rose whispered.

Cassidy had barely heard her.

"Stop," Rose repeated.

Cassidy froze in the dense patch of woods. "What's wrong?"

"Do you hear that?"

Cassidy's instincts were usually finely tuned, but she hadn't heard anything except the roar of the ocean in the background and the rustle of the leaves as the branches clapped together in the breeze.

"Someone's out there," Rose whispered. "Get behind the tree."

Cassidy almost refused. Rose had to be wrong. No one was out here right now but them.

She slid behind a tree anyway, flinching as the rough bark cut into her fingertips. A moment later, headlights cut through the darkness.

Rose was right. Someone was out there.

And nothing good was going to come from this.

Chapter Eleven

"IT'S the men who are looking for us," Rose whispered, her breath coming out as a hiss. "I just know it. Did you call someone?"

Cassidy's chest tightened with tension, irritation, and pure fighting instinct. "You've been with me the whole time. You know I didn't."

Rose glared at her, the look so searing it nearly lit up the darkness around them. "How did they find us then?"

"I have no idea." Cassidy swatted a bug lingering around her neck, wishing they could keep moving. "And why are these men even looking for you?"

"You don't want to know."

The unease in Cassidy's gut grew by the moment. Something was seriously wrong here. Something bad.

She peered out from behind the tree, wishing the branches weren't blocking her view, yet grateful they concealed her.

"We need to get closer to see what they're doing," Cassidy said.

Rose squeezed her arm. "No, they'll see us."

"I'll be careful. I promise." Cassidy set down her bags and crept forward.

Sure enough, a dark sedan slinked down the lane.

Was the driver looking for the women?

Most vacationers weren't out this late. Lantern Beach didn't have that kind of nightlife. No, it was mostly a family town.

The car stopped near Rose's cottage.

"No, no, no . . ." Rose seemed to grind her teeth beside her.

"Just hold tight," Cassidy whispered, her arm jutting out to prevent Rose from doing anything foolish.

"Who are you? Wonder Woman?"

"No, I'm the Ice Cream Woman." She glanced at Rose. "That was supposed to be funny."

"Well, Ice Cream Woman . . . you're going to get us killed. And keep your day job. Please."

The car door opened, and a man stepped out. Cassidy couldn't make out his features in the darkness. If only the moon was full, maybe they'd have a chance. But tonight it was just a sliver in the sky.

"No . . ." Rose whispered.

Cassidy squatted on the ground and felt around. Sand. A thorny vine. More bark.

Finally, she found a rock—a good-sized one, at

that. She pulled her arm back, remembering all those softball pitching lessons she'd been through.

"What are you doing?" Rose asked.

"Trust me."

"I don't even know you."

"Just watch."

And before Rose could argue anymore, Cassidy tossed the rock toward the house across the street. She held her breath, waiting to see if her plan worked.

A minute later, the motion-activated sprinkler came on, followed by floodlights.

The man quickly got back into his car. Two seconds later, he backed down the lane, sufficiently spooked.

"How'd you know?" Rose asked.

"Because I sold ice cream to that family earlier."

"Well, that was a lucky throw."

Cassidy shrugged. "What can I say? Either way, we need to get to your friends. They're not going to be safe staying there much longer."

Just as Cassidy leaned down to retrieve the bags, Rose whipped forward and grabbed the gun from Cassidy's waistband.

Cassidy sighed. She should have known better.

"Who are you, really?" Rose said. "You work for the Cobra, don't you?"

The Cobra? That was the name that had been written on that paper. "Who's the Cobra?"

"He's the man who did all of this."

"I don't work for him. I'm telling you the truth. I just sell ice cream."

"I'm not some dopey suburban kid or naïve islander. There's more to your story."

Cassidy's heart pounded into her ribcage. "I don't know what else to tell you. I do know that I just scared away someone who obviously shook you up. If I was involved with this, why would I do that? Why would I bring you food and clothes?"

Rose stared at her. "That's what I'm trying to figure out."

"Please, let's get the medicine to your friend. Then we can sort all of this out."

"I'm keeping the gun."

"Fine." Cassidy would rather have the gun herself, especially if that driver came back. But she'd deal with this one step at a time.

They scrambled back toward the house, looking up and down the lane for any sign of that car. It was gone.

But they might not have much time before it returned.

Cassidy raised a water bottle to the lips of the woman lying on the couch. She gulped down the liquid, hardly taking time to breathe.

"What's your name?" Cassidy asked, noting the woman's pale skin.

"Don't tell her," Rose barked. "The less she knows, the better."

"What can it hurt if she tells me her first name?" Cassidy said. "I already heard you say Trina's name."

The plump, injured woman took the aspirin from Cassidy's hand and took another long sip of water. Then her weary gaze went to Rose.

"I'm Kat," she said, raising her chin with a touch of defiance.

"I'm Cassidy." She glanced back at Rose, making sure the woman understood what Cassidy was about to say. "You guys can't stay here."

"We have nowhere else to go." Rose crossed her arms, Cassidy's gun still in her hand.

"You can come to my place." Cassidy questioned her offer as soon as it left her lips. Yet she didn't take the words back. No, these women needed somewhere safe to hide, and her house was as good as any. She'd have to deal with the repercussions of her offer later.

"I think we should do it," Trina said, scarfing down some crackers and a diet soda. "It's like you said. The car could come back. We can't risk it."

"I still don't trust her." Rose didn't bother to disguise her wariness towards Cassidy. "She's hiding something. I can see it in her eyes. This could all be a trap."

"If this was a trap, you'd already be caught." Cassidy had to admit that the woman had enough street smarts to unnerve her. Of all the people Cassidy had met, Rose had the most potential to unearth the truth about Cassidy's past. And she'd just invited the woman into her home. "I don't know how else to convince you. There's nothing in this for me."

Cassidy stood and waited.

Rose remained quiet, her narrowed eyes still on Cassidy.

Cassidy couldn't stay here all night trying to convince them. She needed to force their decision. "You know what? Forget it. You can all stay here. I'm not going to twist your arms and make you do anything you're not comfortable with. I just need my gun back, and I'll be going."

Cassidy held out her hand, waiting for Rose to hand it over. Rose continued to stare at her.

"Rose . . ." Kat's voice cracked with desperation. "You know we need help. We're not going to make it much longer here on our own. We have no money, no car, no food. Nothing. Besides, this place is hot and dirty, and we have no running water."

Rose slowly shook her head. "If those guys find us . . ."

"I think we can trust her," Trina added. "What choice do we have? Besides, Kat needs help. Maybe more help than we can give her. What good does it do to escape from the Cobra but to die while hiding out?"

Whatever the story was behind these women showing up here, it grew more and more intriguing. Cassidy hoped they'd share it soon. And she hoped they'd accept her help.

Cassidy nodded. "Your friend needs a safer—cleaner—place to recover."

"I say we do it, Rose." Trina's gaze implored Rose.

"Quiet!" Rose began pacing the kitchen, her shoes making a sticking sound each time they touched the floor. "I need to think."

Cassidy edged closer to the door. "Well, I'm out of here. I just need my gun."

"I don't want to give you this gun," Rose snapped. "Might need it."

"No, I might need it, and it's registered to me." Cassidy had actually scraped off the serial number, but no one else needed to know that.

Rose paused, her nostrils flaring. With a touch of hesitancy, she stretched out her arm and handed the gun back to Cassidy

"Fine," Rose said, her voice low. "We'll go with you. But don't make me regret it, Ice Cream Woman."

Cassidy hid a smile. Maybe slowly but surely the woman would trust her. Maybe.

"We should get moving before that car comes back," Cassidy said. "Let's go."

Back at Cassidy's house, she put Kat and Trina into the spare bedroom with twin beds. Rose would stay in the third bedroom, the one with the queen-sized bed, but the woman didn't appear ready to sleep. Cassidy really wanted to talk to her and find out more information, if she would open up.

And that was a big *if.*

It was nearly morning anyway, and sleep wouldn't be happening for Cassidy. Thankfully, she'd learned to survive on little rest during her beat-cop days.

Rose hadn't eaten back at the house—she'd let the other ladies have the snacks. That had to be a sign that she wasn't all rough edges. So Cassidy fixed her a sandwich and pushed it toward her.

Rose hadn't said anything, just eaten it quickly, gulping down two bottles of water as she did.

"Do you want to fill me in?" Cassidy sat across the dining room table from her, tamping down her need for answers.

"The less you know, the better." She took another bite.

Cassidy noted the vast difference between how Rose looked now and how she'd looked in the pictures online. The woman almost looked emaciated.

"It's going to be hard for me to help you if I don't know details," Cassidy finally said.

"You can help us by not telling anyone we're here."

"I already told you I wouldn't." Cassidy stared at the woman, who wiped her mouth with the back of her hand then took another long sip of water. "You were on that raft that washed ashore, weren't you?"

Rose didn't say anything, which meant yes.

Cassidy rubbed the edge of the table where a piece of the vinyl overlay had bubbled. "What kind of circumstance made you go to such desperate lengths?"

Rose's gaze fluttered up to hers again before hardening as she turned back to her food. "You wouldn't understand."

Cassidy knew she'd never convince her with lies. Instead, she said, "You don't have to talk to me, Rose. It's not a prerequisite for you staying here. But I have no intention of hurting you in any way. I'm just a simple island girl who sells ice cream and happens to carry a gun for my protection. I know a thing or two about how evil mankind can be. I've seen it firsthand. I've lived it out. So if you want to talk, I'm here, and I'd be more than happy to try and help in any way I can. You seem like you could use all the help you could get right now."

Rose only grunted.

"To be honest, I got involved with some bad people. It's one of the reasons I came here. I had to get away and turn my life around."

Rose stared at the table a minute before looking up, that same defiant look in her eyes. Cassidy was sure she was going to remain silent.

To her surprise, Rose said, "We were abducted. All three of us."

Cassidy's heart pounded harder. "I'm . . . sorry to hear that."

"This man kept us on an island. They called him

the Cobra. He was going to sell us to the highest bidder. He made that clear."

Cassidy's stomach churned. "But then . . ."

"But then we escaped." Rose's face tightened. "We washed ashore. Here, of all places."

Cassidy tilted her head. "What do you mean?"

"I heard the Cobra talking about this place. Apparently, he comes here to do business. I don't know how regularly. I just know this was the last place we wanted to wash up. Virginia Beach . . . we might have had a chance to blend in. But I'm afraid he'll find us here."

"So you actually heard him mention Lantern Beach?" Cassidy clarified.

"That's right. He had some business here. He also mentioned stopping in Myrtle Beach."

"I guess you found that abandoned house after you washed ashore," Cassidy said, trying to put together a mental timeline.

"That's right. We knew that the Cobra was going to try and track us down. He thinks of us as property. Valuable property. Do you know how much money he can make off one of us? A lot. Unlike drugs, he can keep selling us over and over again."

Cassidy wanted to reach across the table and grab her hand. But she couldn't. The action would only scare Rose.

"That's horrible, Rose. But I don't understand why we can't go to the police with this. They can help you."

She forcefully shook her head, her walls reassembling at record speed. "You don't know anything."

"Then tell me. Help me see."

Rose leaned closer. "Cassidy, the police are a part of this whole scheme. They say they'll help, but they'll really just sell us right back into the life we escaped."

Chapter Twelve

14 WEEKS EARLIER

CADY COULDN'T STOP THINKING about the sound she'd heard in the building at DH-7's headquarters.

If Sloan hadn't caught her hovering outside the doorway, Cady would have checked it out.

Since then, she'd been waiting for the right time and the right opportunity.

That chance came the next day when most of the DH-7 members went to confront a rival gang in the deep recess of the night. Cady had a different assignment—she needed to deliver some drugs to a dealer across town. And she would to keep her cover. However, there was something she needed to do first.

She waited fifteen minutes after they left before she made her move.

Then Cady went down the hallway and found that same door.

The same tap sounded, like someone was sending an SOS.

After looking up and down the hallway for signs of anyone watching, Cady twisted the handle. It was locked. Of course.

But she'd expected that, and she'd come prepared. From her pocket, she pulled out two metal rods she'd found in an old tool box and began working them within the lock. A moment later, a click sounded.

She'd done it. The door was unlocked.

Just as she was about to push the door open, a footstep echoed in the distance.

She shoved the tools back into her pocket and slipped inside the doorway across the hall. An old janitor's closet that smelled like bleach surrounded her. Something scampered across her feet.

She held back a gasp.

Through the crack, she watched.

Sloan paced past.

Her heart pounded harder. Why had he stayed behind and not gone with everyone else?

He kept walking, but his gaze indicated he was looking for something. Someone.

Cady?

Her heart pounded harder. What if he was onto her? If he'd come to find her, to torture her until the truth bled out along with her life force?

She'd known when she accepted this assignment that it could turn deadly. But facing death . . . it wasn't something she was prepared for. She still had too much life left.

Besides, she hadn't even found Lucy's killer, her

whole reason for becoming a cop. Her best friend needed justice.

The footsteps faded. She waited three full minutes, counting out each second, until she finally opened the door and scanned the corridor.

Sloan was gone.

She slipped out and hurried across the hall. She didn't have the luxury of hesitating this time. Her hand went to the knob, and she twisted it. The door opened, and Cady slipped inside the space.

Her eyes slowly adjusted to the darkness.

But what she saw made her want to lose her lunch.

It was a roomful of women. Six of them.

And each were chained like prisoners to a pipe running across the center of the wall.

Chapter Thirteen

TODAY'S GOALS: HELP THESE WOMEN. FIND
ANSWERS ABOUT THE COBRA. BUY MORE ICE CREAM.

CASSIDY HADN'T SLEPT all night. No, she'd stayed
on the couch and run everything through her mind
repeatedly.

These poor women. She couldn't even imagine
everything they'd been through. She only knew one
thing: she needed to keep them safe and assist them in
finding the help they needed.

All the while maintaining a low profile herself.
That was one of the hardest tasks of them all.

As the sun began to rise, Cassidy stepped onto her
deck with a cup of coffee in hand. The day would be
another scorcher. In fact, it was already downright hot
outside.

In her fitful, pathetic attempt to rest, all she'd been
able to think about were Rose, Trina, and Kat.

Who could be behind the abduction of these

women? Someone with power. Someone who knew this area. Someone who probably wasn't whom he seemed.

Her mind raced through the possibilities. Could it be Martin Chaser, the racecar driver? Smith Anderson, the TV personality who just happened to be in town and possibly trying to build a hotel against the wishes of the locals? Or what about the parade coordinator, Niles Something-or-other? According to Serena, he'd shown an unusual interest in the raft.

Cassidy didn't know, but all three of those men seemed worth checking out.

As she leaned against the railing, her phone buzzed. She looked down at the screen and saw that it was Ty. Her heart jumped with excitement, followed quickly by dread.

Again, the familiar questions haunted her. Had Ty told Renee he loved her, as Renee had claimed? That the two of them deserved to be together? Did Renee have anything to do with Ty's silence when he'd left for six days without telling Cassidy why?

Cassidy knew one thing: modern dating was the pits. If she was smart, she would be content to simply remain single the rest of her life.

And she might have been okay with that.

Before she met Ty.

She read his message.

Ty: Hi

Cassidy stared at her phone. It seemed so out of

character for Ty to text something so . . . casual. Despite that, she typed back: How are you feeling?

That seemed safe and noncommittal enough.

Ty: I've been better.

Cassidy: Good thing Renee is there to take care of you.

Cassidy's stomach turned as she typed the words. She wasn't one for relationship drama, but she hadn't been able to resist the quip.

Ty: It's not like you think.

Maybe that was Cassidy's problem. She'd thought too much. Assumed too much. Let her heart roam a little too freely.

Cassidy: It's none of my business.

But, oh did she want to know! What was their story? What was going on in Ty's head?

Ty: Can we talk sometime?

Cassidy didn't want to get into the middle of anything. But Ty was her friend.

Her emotions churned inside her. Cassidy was just going to have to take the mature route here. Act like the friend she'd agreed to be.

Finally, she typed back: Of course. I just don't want to make your fiancée uncomfortable.

Ty: You're impossible.

Cassidy: And I'm impressed with your grammatical texting skills. You know the difference between you're and your. Keep up the good work.

She couldn't resist the jab. Besides, jabs helped her

to maintain her emotional distance—and she needed that right now.

Ty: Your so funny.

Cassidy read his intentional mistake and shook her head. At least he still had his sense of humor.

Cassidy: Good one. We'll go over there, they're, and their later.

Ty: I'm looking forward to it.

Cassidy smiled and typed: You convinced me. I'll stop by later. Do you need anything?

Ty: My sanity.

Cassidy: I can't help you with that.

Ty: You might be surprised.

She smiled again and slipped her phone back into her pocket.

She'd go visit him sometime during her ice cream route this morning. But first she wanted to talk to Rose again.

***

Rose wandered from her room an hour later looking a little more rested and not quite as rough around the edges. At least for the moment.

Cassidy sensed a brokenness about the woman. She recognized it because that same brokenness lingered inside her also. Only Cassidy didn't display it by getting in trouble or rebelling. No, she'd dealt with it by continually pushing herself to be the best. With sleepless nights where the minutes ticked by and made her wonder how she could have done things better. How she could do life better.

Casting those thoughts aside, Cassidy stood from the couch where she'd been writing out a grocery list. "Can I make you some breakfast? Bacon and eggs?"

Rose's eyes lit as hunger temporarily broke down her walls. "Don't go out of your way."

Cassidy took that as a yes.

The woman reminded Cassidy of a caged pit bull she'd once rescued from a house. The dog had seemed ferocious at first, but all it took was some food and a little loving before the dog warmed up and lost the wild look in its eyes.

Despite that thought, Cassidy couldn't help but notice the knife protruding from the back pocket of the woman's jeans. She had to remain on guard.

Rose sat at the breakfast bar as Cassidy began pulling out some pans.

"How'd you sleep?" Cassidy asked, trying to make conversation.

Rose raked a hand through her mop of long, dark hair and scowled. "None of your business."

"That's good to hear." Cassidy pretended the woman hadn't made the jab. Instead, she grabbed the butter, eggs, and bacon from the fridge. "Have you checked on Kat? I didn't want to wake her."

She expected her to say "mind your own business" again. Instead, Rose said, "She's sleeping like a baby."

"That's great news." Cassidy filled the pan with strips of bacon and listened to them sizzle. As they continued to cook, she poured Rose a cup of coffee. "Cream and sugar?"

"Just black."

Cassidy drew in a deep breath before launching into her next question. The chances of getting an answer were fifty-fifty. "Do you have relatives looking for you, Rose?"

The lines on her face grew more rigid. "Why do you want to know?"

"Because I have to ask questions and get some answers to figure out how to best help you."

She said nothing for a minute. As she waited, the scent of bacon made Cassidy's own stomach grumble, even though she'd eaten an hour ago.

"My family doesn't really care," Rose finally said.

"I can understand that."

Rose snorted. "I'm sure you can."

"No, I really can. My parents relegated my care to nannies and strangers. If I disappeared . . . they probably wouldn't notice for a while." The admission was probably too honest, but Cassidy said it anyway.

In fact, her parents hadn't noticed. It had taken more than a month. Then they'd hired her ex-boyfriend to find her.

Cassidy was still trying to come to terms with all of it.

Cassidy hadn't intended on sharing all of that with Rose, but now that she had, she hoped it didn't come back to bite her later.

"How about the other ladies?" Cassidy flipped the bacon, trying to sound casual.

"You're not a cop, are you?"

Cassidy's shoulders tensed. "Why would you ask that?"

"You give off that vibe."

"Funny, you're the first person who's ever said that. Most people always said I'd never amount to anything. If I was lucky maybe I'd get an athletic scholarship. Look at me now. I'm selling ice cream." Her sarcasm lingered in the air.

Cassidy's heart pounded in her chest. Had she pulled off the ploy? Did Rose buy it?

Rose frowned again. "We all come from broken families. Even if we wanted to, we couldn't contact them. Not until the Cobra is behind bars. He threatened our families. If we run to them now . . ."

"You'll put everyone in danger," Cassidy finished.

"Exactly."

Cassidy understood that a little too well. "What can you tell me about this Cobra guy?"

Rose snorted again. "What, are you going to go track him down?"

Well . . . maybe. But she wouldn't admit it to Rose. "I have connections here in town. I can keep my eyes open for you. We know he's looking for you. Maybe we can beat him to it."

"You don't want to find him." Rose swung her head back and forth, leaving no questions about her stance on the matter.

"I'm sure I don't. But I'd still like to know who to watch out for. Did you see his face?"

Rose took a quick chug of coffee. "Only parts of it, enough to know he was a white man. On the taller side. He had a fit build."

"Hair?"

"He always wore hats and sunglasses, so it was hard to tell. He did have a coiled cobra tattoo on his left bicep."

That was something, at least.

"Is there anything else? Anything at all?" Cassidy needed more to go on. "Did he walk with a limp or have a chipped tooth or have any strange catchphrases?"

"You sound like you've done this before, Ice Cream Woman." A touch of distrust entered Rose's gaze.

Cassidy turned away, lifting the bacon from the pan with tongs and putting it on some paper towels. "I don't know what to say. I like solving problems, I guess. You might have noticed that I like to read mystery novels. Maybe I let them get into my head too much."

Cassidy had bought a whole stack at a used bookstore, just to keep up her cover.

"Seems like you might be pretty good at it."

"I'm not. I have no idea what I'm doing. I only know that we didn't meet by accident."

Rose sighed, seeming to chew on Cassidy's words. "I don't know. I tried not to pay attention to him. I just know he was mean and greedy. Oh, and he likes liver and onions."

"Liver and onions?" Of all the things Rose could notice, that seemed like a strange one.

"I could smell it on him." Rose scrunched her nose. "My foster parents used to always make them when I was a kid, and I'd remember the scent anywhere."

Well, it was something.

Cassidy began frying up some eggs. Her mom had been more of a yogurt and granola type. Fried eggs in particular were something for the uncultured, not for society's most elite and wealthy. Honestly, they were some of Cassidy's favorites. The gooey insides. . . mixed with some salty bacon . . . with some toast for dipping.

It was her guilty pleasure.

"I know he has money—and he loves money," Rose continued. "He'd do anything for it."

"And this island where he kept you . . . can you tell me anything else about it? How big it was? Where exactly it was located?"

"I was in Charleston when I disappeared." She frowned and looked away. "I was supposed to hook up with this guy I met online. He seemed great. I thought he might be too good to be true, but I needed to meet him and find out for myself."

Cassidy had heard these stories one too many times before. She knew exactly where it was going but braced herself anyway.

"We had coffee together, and I was blown away." Rose frowned, obviously not the type who was used to getting taken. "He was amazing. I mean, simply amazing. We decided to go to a movie. That was my mistake. I got into the car with him. That's when he pulled out a gun and took me to a marina instead."

"Was it the Cobra?"

"No, it was one of the men he has who helps him with the dirty work." She frowned. "He tied me up and covered my eyes. The next thing I knew, I was on this island with two other women."

"I'm sorry, Rose." Cassidy's voice softened with compassion.

The woman still didn't make eye contact. "The place was pretty small. You could see water from any window. It wasn't the Caribbean. At least, I don't think so. I've never been. But the water didn't look turquoise like it does in all them ads on TV. But I couldn't see land either."

"How did you get away?" Cassidy asked.

"They left for three days—told us they were going and left us a supply of food and water. We saw our opportunity. We knew we had to get off and get off then. We picked the lock to our room and looked for a phone. There were none. We looked for a boat—anything that could float. We didn't find anything, so we decided to make our own."

"How did you even know which direction to go once you managed to make the boat—out of a twin bed and Styrofoam? Very impressive, by the way." She flipped the eggs. They were almost ready.

"I may not have graduated from high school, but I know the sun goes down in the west. That's the way we headed."

"Good for you. And how many days were you adrift?"

"Three nights. Four days. The waters were getting rough, and we didn't think we'd ever make it to dry land. We were saying our prayers. And then we washed up here."

Someone who was skilled on the water could probably calculate where the current would drop them off.

So there was a good chance that car last night had been the Cobra—or the Cobra's men, at least. It was like Rose had said—he was looking for his property. With the amount these ladies were "worth," he'd go to great lengths to find them. It took time to cultivate enough relationships to replace his "inventory."

"You can't tell anyone we're here." Rose's gaze finally latched onto Cassidy's. "You've got to promise me, Ice Cream Woman."

Cassidy chewed on her bottom lip a moment. Not telling anyone would make it more challenging to find this Cobra guy. But she understood the woman's concern and nodded. "I won't. Just do me a favor and stay low. If the Cobra knows you're here, he's going to keep looking, and I don't want to do anything to give away your presence."

Rose nodded. "I get that. And thanks for letting us stay in your crib."

"You're welcome." Cassidy slid a plate of food in front of Rose, feeling like maybe—maybe—the two of them were finally making some progress. "Now eat up."

Chapter Fourteen

CASSIDY LEFT Rose in charge while she was gone, and the woman promised to fix breakfast for the other ladies.

She had some reservations about leaving strangers in her place, but Cassidy knew she'd covered all her bases. Even if the women snooped, they wouldn't find anything that would point to her past life—except maybe the guns Cassidy had hidden. But she'd made sure they were somewhere no one would discover them.

As far as her valuables . . . well, she didn't have any. All her cash was in her purse, which she kept on her.

She needed to start her ice cream route before too long—and she needed to pick up some new inventory at the marina. She was trying a new service with a wholesaler that sent deliveries over by boat. That was the challenge with island life—nothing was easily accessible, including deliveries. And with the women taking a good portion of Cassidy's food, she was running low.

But first, she stayed true to her word and stopped by the clinic to visit Ty.

No drama, she reminded herself. On the outside or on the inside. But if she ran into Renee again . . . she wasn't sure how everything would go.

Despite her mental reminders, she still felt a swell of tension in her as she approached his door. She gently knocked and prepared herself to see Renee again. To her surprise, she heard Ty call, "Come in."

She pushed the door open, instantly feeling lighter when she saw her friend—even if he was in a hospital bed and wearing an unflattering hospital gown.

Cassidy glanced around. No Renee in sight, but there was plenty of evidence she'd been here. Evidence like the cheerful daisies and the colorful heart blanket folded on the couch and a small turquoise suitcase in the corner.

She closed the door behind her, halfway hoping to shut the woman out for good. If only it was that easy. Besides, Ty might feel differently. Apparently, he *did* feel differently since he was giving their relationship another chance.

Cassidy placed a cinnamon roll in his lap, reminding herself to keep her distance. "From Lisa. It's a little late for breakfast, but maybe you can have it as a snack later."

"You'll have to thank her for me. And did you try those salt-and-vinegar sugar cookies?"

"I conveniently gave them all to you." She shuddered.

"Ask her to make you some. They were out of this world."

"I find that hard to believe." As much as she liked Lisa's weird combinations, that one seemed like too much for even Cassidy.

"I promise." Ty opened the bag and pulled out his breakfast.

Cassidy lowered herself into the seat beside him, an unseen weight pressing on her shoulders. "How are you feeling, Ty?"

"Much better. A hundred percent. They're even talking about letting me go home later today."

Cassidy's eyebrows shot up. "Isn't that soon?"

"Doc Clemson said the way I'm bouncing back is amazing. I just needed some antibiotics."

"That's great news." Cassidy glanced around, the weight returning to her shoulders. "Where's your girlfriend?"

He chuckled—although he didn't sound amused. More like annoyed. "Renee is not my girlfriend."

"Your fiancée?"

"She's not my fiancée, either."

Cassidy clearly remembered the conversation from yesterday. "Are you sure?"

"Am I sure? Of course I'm sure. Why would you even ask that?"

Cassidy licked her lips, trying to choose her words wisely and not sound like a clingy, spurned woman. "Does Renee know that?"

"I've tried to make myself clear over and over again, and I don't seem to be getting through to her."

"You don't seem like the pushover type."

He sighed and pushed his cinnamon roll away. "I'm not, but she has a way of twisting my words. Now she keeps saying she wants to make things right. She changed her wording, even though I think she means the same thing."

"She told me you were getting back together." Cassidy clamped her mouth shut, hoping she hadn't revealed too much.

"She told me you called her deplorable, so obviously she gets things wrong sometimes."

Cassidy cringed. "Well, I didn't exactly call her deplorable. I called her actions deplorable."

Ty's eyes widened. "You did what?"

"I'm sorry but she pranced out there, talking about how you loved her, and she wanted to move to Atlanta, and I got a little overprotective."

Ty stared at her, and Cassidy waited for the lecture. She'd been out of line. She knew it then, and she knew it now. To her surprise, a chuckle filled the air.

"I can't believe you said that," Ty said.

"I'm sorry."

"Don't be sorry. She needed to hear it and get a good dose of reality. There's forgiveness, and then there's forgiveness. I just can't seem to get through to her that forgiving doesn't necessarily equate to getting back together."

Cassidy released a breath, unreasonably happy to learn the truth. "Where is Renee now?"

"She wanted to take a morning walk on the beach. She's decided that she loves Lantern Beach, and that it's much nicer than Virginia Beach."

"That's where you were when you two met?"

He nodded. "Yeah, that's where I was stationed. She lives in Minnesota now. Please say you believe me when I say I didn't ask her to come."

"I believe you."

He grabbed her hand. "I'd much rather you be here."

Cassidy's cheeks flushed at the emotion behind his words.

Build those walls back up, Cassidy, she reminded herself. *Falling for Ty will only bring you trouble.*

She cleared her throat and felt a gleam in her eyes. "Well, maybe it's a good thing she showed up. I'm a terrible nurse. At least Renee had three months of experience while in school."

"I have a hard time believing that you'd be a bad nurse. You seem to do well at whatever you put your mind to."

She shrugged, desperate not to let him see how much she cared—and how much she wanted to be here. "And I have some extremely demanding customers who really want their snow cones and ice pops every day."

"Now that I can believe."

"Reports of how delightful my icy cold sweet treats are have not been exaggerated. I'm very much in demand."

Ty's eyes were like two pools that tried to pull Cassidy into their abyss, leaving her without escape. "I know at least one person that's true for. However, I look like a zombie and I'm doped up, so this is no time to pretend to be Prince Charming."

"I agree. Plus your ex-fiancée is here."

His face darkened. "Don't remind me."

"Your ex-fiancée is here."

His eyes narrowed. "Really?"

"I'm just trying to make the best of a strange situation."

"Tell me what's going on with you. Please. I heard you found a raft that washed ashore."

"How'd you hear that?"

"Mac stopped by."

Mac. Of course.

Her heart lurched. If only she could tell Ty everything that was going on. But she couldn't. So she told him what she could, stopping short of her discovery of the women.

"So do you think it's refugees?"

Cassidy shook her head. "No, I think there were people on board who were desperate to get away from something—or someone."

"If that's true, where are they?"

At my house. She bit the words back. "Hiding out somewhere on the island would be my guess."

"Do you think they're still in danger?"

"It's a very real possibility."

"I have a guess also—you're looking into it, aren't you?"

Cassidy shrugged. "Why would I do that?"

"Because you can't help yourself."

"Looking into it would be extreme. I'm just keeping my eyes open."

"Well, be safe. Please."

She nodded. Ty knew her better than she assumed. "I will."

As the door opened, Cassidy withdrew her hand from Ty's.

Renee stepped inside, a huge smile on her face. Her cheeks were rosy with exertion, and her hair looked victim of the area's humidity. No longer did it look perfect and bouncy. Oh, no, frizzies had started to set in.

Cassidy found just a touch of satisfaction in that knowledge.

"Oh, it's you. The neighbor. It's so good to see you again." Renee rushed over to Ty's bedside, practically shoving Cassidy out of the way with her hip. "I brought you some oatmeal, Ty Ty."

Cassidy smiled. Ty hated oatmeal. It was a texture thing, he'd said.

And this was her cue to leave, despite the way Ty's

eyes pleaded with her. Renee was one problem Ty was going to have to deal with on his own.

———

Cassidy caught Doc Clemson in the hallway before she left. He was whistling and doing a little dance with a life-sized plastic skeleton while the nurses—his audience—laughed. It was no wonder he and Mac got along so well.

"Do you have time for a quick question?" she asked. "When you're done dancing?"

"I'm about to eat lunch. If you don't mind watching me eat, you can ask then."

"I don't mind at all." Cassidy followed him down the short hallway to an office tucked into the back of the building.

"It's been a busy day with tourist injuries. The ocean is one big bully lately," he said as she followed him. "People have stepped on broken shells and cut their feet. They've gotten tossed by waves. They've had terrible cases of I-Forgot-to-Use-Sunscreenitis."

"Sounds awful." Cassidy smiled and followed him into his office. She glanced at a picture on his bookshelf. It was of Clemson in surgery, holding a . . . brain? She didn't ask.

"So how are you doing, Cassidy Livingston? Are you enjoying life here in Lantern Beach?" he asked over his shoulder.

"I am. It's really nice here." She slipped into the

chair on the other side of his desk. He grabbed a brown paper bag from a mini fridge, sat in his chair, and pulled out a sandwich and fruit, all neatly packed.

"Well, it's been an interesting summer between the man who was murdered, the drug ring that was busted, and now this raft that's washed ashore."

"It has been interesting," Cassidy agreed, watching her tongue. Doc Clemson and Mac both were the types who made it way too easy to talk. If Cassidy wasn't careful, she'd pour out her whole story to one of them.

"Now, what can I do for you?" He took a bite of his sandwich.

"I'm curious. I have a question about sailing, and someone told me you were the person to talk to."

"It's one of my favorite pastimes."

"I'm trying to figure out how far a boat would . . . float . . . in four days in the ocean."

"You mean sail?"

She shook her head. "What if the sail was somehow broken?"

"And there's not a backup motor?"

Cassidy shook her head. "Nope."

He took a bite of his sandwich and chewed thoughtfully before answering. "There are a lot of factors involved here, everything from the wind, to the currents, to what's going on out in the ocean."

"I suspected that. I was hoping you could ballpark it."

He studied her more closely. "Does this have anything to do with that raft?"

She waved a hand in the air. "Don't be silly. Who knows where that came from? Probably Cuba."

He nodded slowly, and Cassidy wasn't sure if he believed her or not. "Well, hypothetically speaking, a boat could cover a lot of ground—water, I should say —in four days. Would it be coming from the north or south?"

"Let's say the south."

He pulled something from his drawer. It was a nautical chart. "Objects usually deflect to the right in the northern hemisphere."

She gave him a questioning look.

"It has to do with something called geostrophic currents. I can explain if you'd like, or you can trust me on it."

"I'll trust you."

"Good choice. Anyway, if you were to start down in Florida, off the coast, the current would naturally want to carry you out into the ocean. In fact, some people claim that there are vessels out there that have been afloat for centuries."

"Really?" Cassidy found that hard to believe, but Clemson seemed to know what he was talking about.

"It's true. But that's neither here nor there. On a day with moderate wind and average ocean currents, I'd guess a vessel set adrift would make it about ten miles."

"Ten miles? That's . . . not very impressive."

"However, I do need to add that the ocean had been stirred up lately, so I'm willing to say in four days —recently—that vessel might even travel twenty miles a day."

"So eighty miles?" Cassidy asked.

He nodded. "Between forty and eighty. It's really hard to predict."

She glanced at his map. "So what's between forty and eighty miles south of here?"

"Anywhere from Cape Lookout to Topsail. Maybe even down to Wilmington."

"Good to know."

"I hope that helps."

She nodded. "It really does. Thank you so much."

She added more facts to her mental list of suspects, motives, and clues. Every little bit she discovered helped, and she never knew when one piece of information might be exactly what she was looking for to solve the case.

"That's right. Do you think you can do that?"

Serena shrugged, her eyelids still fluttering. "I guess I can try. But why do you want to see that raft so bad?"

"It's just a hunch," was all Cassidy could offer.

Serena pushed up her oversized glasses. Today, the girl had dressed in homage to Lois Lane with her hair pulled into a bun, glasses, and a dark suit. However, they were on Lantern Beach, so the suit consisted of pressed shorts and a quarter-sleeve blazer.

Strangely, Serena pulled off the look.

Life was never boring when that girl was around.

They pulled up to the station, and the receptionist ushered them back to Quinton. His eyes lit when he saw them.

"If it isn't Chastity."

Cassidy scowled and didn't bother to correct him this time. Thankfully, Serena jumped in. "I'm with the *Lantern Outlook*, and I'd really love to see that raft that washed ashore."

He stared, a halfway stupefied look on his face. "Why?"

"Because this is one of the most exciting things to happen on the island since . . . since . . ." Serena's voice trailed off.

"That drug bust a few weeks ago," Cassidy finished.

Quinton nodded, as if the explanation made sense. "The raft really isn't a big deal. After the Coast

Guard looks at it, it'll probably be sent to the waste management facilities. You know, the landfill."

"Then it's not a big deal if we see it?" Cassidy batted her eyelashes for extra effect.

Quinton grinned that dopey grin he always sported when a pretty girl gave him attention. "I probably should run it past the chief."

"Where is he?" Cassidy twirled her hair again, a little more of her self-respect dying a cold, hard death.

Quinton shrugged. "Someone tagged his car."

"What do you mean?" Serena asked.

"You know, they spray-painted it," Quinton said. "Wrote Bozo on it. He's pretty sensitive about that."

"Then maybe it's best if we don't bother him," Cassidy said. "He has more important things to worry about right now. I'm sure he trusts the decisions of his very capable officers."

Quinton's shoulders seemed to poof at her compliment. "I guess you can look at it real quick—before the Coast Guard gets here."

"The Coast Guard hasn't seen it yet?" Surprise rippled through Cassidy at the announcement.

Quinton shrugged. "They weren't too interested at first—especially since there was no body on board. But we got a call last night saying they'd be coming by."

It sounded like Cassidy and Serena were just in time.

"We'll be quick," Cassidy said.

Serena raised her camera. "Just a few pictures. You'll never know we were here."

"Well, I can't see where it would hurt anything." Quinton shrugged and motioned for them to follow.

They scrambled behind him, down the hallway and out a door at the back of the building. A fenced-off area greeted them, and in the center of the cement block sat the raft.

As waves of heat rose from the ground around them, they walked toward the vessel. In the background, Cassidy could hear a band—maybe the local high school?—practicing for the Fourth of July, the sound of *America the Beautiful* stretching through the air.

While Serena snapped photos, Cassidy scanned the inside. Finding a locket in this thing would require a near miracle. Most likely, the piece of jewelry had fallen out. Even if it hadn't, Cassidy couldn't exactly climb aboard the vessel since it was on a trailer. The whole thing looked like it would collapse if the wind blew in the right direction.

Now that Cassidy knew the story behind it, seeing it did something to her. She imagined Rose, Trina, and Kat piecing this together out of things they found at the house. She imagined the bravery it took for them to put this in the ocean and set adrift, unsure where they would end up. Only knowing that anywhere was better than that island.

Cassidy had to help them. Investigating was just so much harder without the resources only accessible to professionals. Then there was also the fact that she didn't want to blow her cover.

"This is some boat, huh?" Quinton said. "You wouldn't catch me in this thing in the ocean. No way. It would be like a floating coffin, in my opinion. Don't quote me on that."

"Maybe being in this boat was a better alternative to staying where they were," Cassidy said.

"Better than *who* staying where they were?" Quinton asked.

"Whoever was inside." Seriously how this guy had ever made it through the police academy was beyond Cassidy's comprehension.

"What's going on here?" a deep voice said behind them.

Cassidy turned and saw a man in a Coast Guard uniform standing there. The man looked like the in-charge type, especially with that scowl on his face and his square jaw raised high in the air.

Quinton's eyes grew large, and he straightened until he was as stiff as a corpse. "Chief Petty Officer Savage?"

"That's right. And who are all of you?" Savage's gaze pierced each of them.

Cassidy had faced far more intimidating men and come out alive to prove it.

"We're from the local newspaper," Cassidy said, since no one else was talking. "This is more exciting than most of the stuff that happens here in a year. We're used to Dale Johnson's truck getting stuck in soft sand while four-wheeling or stories about anglers who let the big one get away."

Savage's gaze darkened even more. "Maybe you should stick to those stories. I didn't approve of this being released to the media."

"We weren't aware you had to approve of anything. We just thought this was something the ocean spit out."

"We don't know anything about this raft yet. And that's why a story in the newspaper is a bad idea." He glanced at Quinton. "Now, I'd really like to inspect this."

"Of course," Quinton said, his cheeks reddening. "Ladies, I'm going to have to ask you to leave."

Cassidy frowned. She hadn't found Trina's necklace. And, at this point, she wouldn't. But at least she'd tried. Somehow, that didn't feel like enough.

"Well, did you get what you wanted?" Serena said as they sat in Cassidy's sedan outside the police station.

Cassidy shrugged, watching as a truck full of fireworks drove by. "I can't say I did."

"That Coast Guard guy was pretty cute."

"If you like the intense type." Serena liked *every* type.

The girl glanced at her watch. "As much as I'd like to sit here and watch you chew on your thoughts, I have another interview I have to do. With Martin Chaser this time."

"Martin Chaser? The racecar driver?"

"He's the one."

Cassidy turned her keys in the ignition, cranked the AC, and pulled onto the highway. "When did he get into town?"

Serena shrugged and tapped her finger against her lip. "That day the boat washed ashore. Why?"

Cassidy tried to piece a timeline together in her head. "When did they ask him to be the grand marshal?"

"When Niles Shepherd—he's the one coordinating the parade—heard Martin was in town, he asked him right then. I guess it was supposed to be Chief Bozeman's father, but he had another engagement that popped up, so he canceled." Serena narrowed her eyes with thought. "Why do you want to know?"

"I'm just trying to figure out how things work here in Lantern Beach."

"Well, good luck with that. Aunt Skye always says this island has more secrets than Alcatraz."

The thought wasn't comforting.

Cassidy pulled to a stop in front of her house and Serena popped out, her car keys in hand.

Cassidy glanced at her watch. The timing was perfect since she had to pick up her inventory.

"It was fun, Cassidy. I'll take over at three!"

Serena yelled over her shoulder. "Wish me luck with Martin Chaser!"

Could Martin Chaser be the Cobra? It was a long shot. But whoever the Cobra was, he had money, power, and connections.

Martin Chaser . . . he was a racecar driver. He lived off taking risks. He'd shown up at just the right time.

He was someone to keep in mind, at least.

But right now, Cassidy needed to switch vehicles and head out to pick up her fudge bars and bomb pops.

Chapter Sixteen
_____

CASSIDY SPOTTED JUST the person she'd hoped
she'd see down at the marina. Jimmy James.

Though Cassidy may have suspected the dock-
worker of being involved in a missing persons case not
too long ago, he also seemed like the type who might
be in the know when it came to shady dealings in the
area. Not to say *he* was shady. At least, he wasn't
supposed to be anymore. That was what Ty had
told her.

She parked Elsa in the lot and hurried from the
vehicle. Thankfully, she had a few minutes to spare
before her own delivery was due. As usual when she
was here, the scent of fish and saltwater and motor oil
mixed in the air, creating a distinct smell she was
likely to never forget. Those things, coupled with the
squawking of birds overhead crying out for food, and
the murmuring of seafarers around her, created a
unique environment. Seattle had its own bigger

version of this with Puget Sound, but this place had a different feel. Quainter, she supposed.

She watched Jimmy James as she approached, noting again that the man had a somewhat amped-up Popeye appearance with his bulging arms and beastly build.

"Hey, there," Cassidy called.

He looked up, recognition lighting his gaze.

"Hey. You're Ty's friend. How's he doing?" Jimmy James asked, unloading some boxes from a large skiff.

"He's hoping to go home today."

"Glad to hear that. What can I do for you?"

"I have a delivery I need to pick up." She casually tucked her hands into her pockets.

"I'll check the clipboard in a minute. Let me just grab a few more of these boxes."

"Sure thing." Cassidy stepped back as more guys unloaded supplies for other area merchants. "I have a question for you. You see any shady characters around here the past couple of days?"

"I work at the docks." His eyes sparkled. "I always see shady characters."

At least he had a sense of humor about it.

"I'm looking for a guy with a cobra tattoo," Cassidy said.

His eyes widened. "I can't say I've seen it."

"Why did you react then?" His eyes had clearly shown recognition.

"No reason."

"Jimmy James . . ." The man's appearance would

rattle most people, but Cassidy had learned not to be intimidated by people. She would have been a terrible detective if she was.

He paused and heaved the box in his hands up higher. "Look, I've heard about a guy who has that tattoo. He calls himself the Cobra."

Her pulse spiked. This might be her first real lead. "When did you hear about him?"

"I haven't always been on the straight and narrow. The Cobra is pretty well-known in some circles. He's a power player. I'd stay away from him if I were you."

"I actually need to find him," Cassidy said.

"Did you just hear a word I said?"

Cassidy shrugged. "I did. But this is important."

"What's so important?"

She'd actually thought this one through. "I heard he ripped off my ice cream truck."

Jimmy James chuckled, and the sound turned into a full-out laugh. "You're joking, right? It's like the person who steals candy from a kid? Certainly he has more important things to do than steal ice cream."

Well . . . that could be true. "No one's going to rip me off, Jimmy James. I want to know who this guy is, and I want to find out if he stole from me."

His smile faded. "I don't know what to tell you. I saw him from a distance."

Why was it that no one ever saw this guy close enough to make out any details? "Is there anything you can tell me about him?"

"He hurt himself. Had a bandage on his arm. That's all I know."

At least it was something. "If you hear anything else, will you let me know?"

"I'll think about it."

She gave him a look.

Jimmy James shrugged. "You're Ty's friend. I don't want to put you in danger. You have no idea who you're dealing with."

She wanted to argue. But she couldn't. Because here she was Cassidy Livingston, the ice cream lady. No one could know that she used to be Cady Matthews, the big-city police detective.

Just then, Elsa started singing "Michael, Row Your Boat Ashore." As always, her timing was impeccable.

Jimmy James chuckled again. "When you going to get that truck fixed?"

Cassidy shrugged. "I'm not sure. She makes life more interesting."

Like she really needed her life to be any more interesting.

"Now, about my ice cream . . ."

With her new supplies loaded into her truck and a few minutes to spare before she needed to start her route, Cassidy pulled out her phone.

She typed Martin Chaser's name into her search engine. She knew it was a long shot that she'd find anything interesting, but she didn't have a lot of options. She was already pushing it with the questions she was asking, and if she wasn't careful, she was going to blow her cover.

Blowing her cover would mean she'd need to leave. Find a new name. A new identity and a new place to stay. It would mean leaving her new friends. Leaving Ty.

The thought caused her heart to twist.

Thankfully, a bunch of headlines filled her screen and distracted her.

She skimmed them, stopping at one halfway down. *Martin Chaser Buying Island off SC Coast.*

South Carolina? That wasn't far from Lantern Beach. Could he have actually bought that island where the women had been kept—and eventually escaped?

Martin moved up higher on her suspect list.

And what did that mean for Serena's upcoming interview with the man? Was she even safe talking to him?

Cassidy wasn't sure. Serena wasn't a girl meeting an online love connection. But she was an impressionable college student who was easily taken in by handsome men.

Cassidy nibbled on her lip as she contemplated what to do. Where was Serena even doing that interview?

Not her place at the campground. Not Ernestine's—the editor's—house. No, Ernestine was too much of a hermit. So where?

Lisa's place, she realized. She would bet Serena was meeting Martin at the Crazy Chefette.

She glanced at her watch. She really should sell ice cream.

But she was going to swing past the restaurant first and ask Lisa to keep an eye on the situation there.

Cassidy sold ice cream for the next three hours. As she did, she searched for the sedan she'd seen last night, but she didn't find it. It had been dark, so the vehicle would be hard to identify. But she'd be remiss if she hadn't at least tried.

The town was all abuzz with tomorrow's upcoming festivities. The police had already started to set up barricades for the parade, and a stage had been erected on the boardwalk, boasting everything red, white, and blue.

Which begged a question in Cassidy's mind . . . what were her limitations during the parade? Could she sell ice cream? Did she need a special permit?

There was only one person she could think to ask: Niles Shepherd.

She smiled at the thought.

Maybe he could clear up some other questions as well. In fact, this made the perfect excuse to talk to him.

She headed down Main Street and stopped at the

municipal center. The receptionist there told her Niles was supervising parade setup downtown and that Cassidy should head there.

Once in the retail district, it wasn't hard to find the man. He must be the one with a whistle around his neck, standing on the sidewalk looking like he was directing traffic. That had to be Niles Shepherd.

Cassidy pulled up beside him in her ice cream truck and offered her most winning smile. "Niles, right?"

He blinked and looked up from his clipboard. "Yes?"

"Someone told me I needed to find you," she started. "I was wondering if I was permitted to sell ice cream tomorrow during the festivities?"

"They told you to find me?" He rolled his eyes. "Of course. My staff evidently cannot make a single decision on their own. What do they think I'm going to do? Cut their heads off if they make a mistake?"

Cassidy would guess that was a very real possibility.

He let out a sigh and snapped his attention to one of his workers. "That banner goes on the other side of the street, you idiot! How many times do I have to tell you?"

Oh. My.

He turned back to her. "I suppose you can sell ice cream." His gaze swiped Elsa and he frowned, as if the truck didn't meet his standards. "As long as you don't get in anyone's way."

"I would never."

As he began yelling out more directions, Cassidy's eyes went to the sleeve of his teal colored Polo. Was that a . . . tattoo peeking out?

Cassidy's breath caught. It was. But was it a cobra?

She scanned his other arm for a sign of injury but didn't see any. Of course, depending on how serious it had been, he could have taken the bandage off.

This might be her only chance to find out if he was her guy.

Think ditzy blonde. Think like someone who's not a detective. Think like anyone but yourself.

That settled it. She knew what she needed to do.

Cassidy gasped loudly—so loudly that Niles jerked his head toward her, his upper lip pulling back in disapproval.

She pretended not to notice and pointed at his arm. "A spider just went up your sleeve."

He looked down, halfway confused, and swatted his arm. When nothing happened, he pulled his sleeve up.

Cassidy's spirits sank. It was a mermaid tattoo.

"I don't see anything," he muttered.

"It must have fallen out when you slapped your arm." She smiled again, making sure her eyes appeared unassuming.

He glared at her. "Anything else?"

"Since you asked, I do have one more question." That was really the last thing Niles wanted, but

Cassidy may as well keep this conversation going for as long as possible. "I know you're busy with the parade and all, but have you heard anything else about that raft that washed up here?"

He looked back at his crew, sweat filling his forehead like an army under the afternoon sun, and then let out the world's longest sigh. "Why would you ask me that? And why right now when you can obviously see I'm busy."

Cassidy pretended again like she didn't notice his irritation. "You seem like someone in the know, Mr. Shepherd. I thought you ran this town. I am the one who found it, and I've been trying to find out some information."

That seemed to appease him. He wiped his forehead with the back of his hand and shrugged. "It's still at the police station. I was hoping they would release it before the parade."

That was curious. "Why's that?"

He gave her a look that made it obvious he thought Cassidy was stupid—just like everyone else in his life. "I wanted to feature it as a way of bringing attention to those less fortunate . . . of course."

"Those less fortunate?" she asked, just wanting a little bit of clarification.

"You know . . . the refugees."

She nodded slowly, purposeful realization dawning over her face. "I see. Good idea."

"I thought it would be nice publicity. But it's not happening. Not now, at least. But maybe later we can bring some additional publicity to Lantern Beach. We need something to boost tourism around here and put this place on the map."

"Or you need someone. Someone like Smith Anderson."

His face reddened. "I don't know what you're talking about."

Oh, but she bet he did.

She didn't say that aloud, though. Instead, she asked, "Can I get you an ice cream sandwich? My treat."

Chapter Seventeen

WHEN CASSIDY GOT BACK to her place, Serena was already waiting in the driveway to start her shift. She leaned against the hood of her sedan, studying her nails and the chipped blue fingernail polish there.

She sat up straight when she saw Cassidy and waved like someone seeing a long-lost friend.

Cassidy pulled her gaze away long enough to note the car in Ty's driveway. That had to be Renee's. Which meant that Ty was probably home.

Cassidy's heart lurched. As much as she wanted to rush over and chat with him, she knew she couldn't—for more than one reason.

"His girlfriend is pretty," Serena said, following her gaze.

Her heart skipped a beat at her pronouncement. "She is."

"She came downstairs a few minutes ago and

talked to me," Serena continued. "Seemed nice enough."

And that was enough of this conversation.

"How'd the interview go?" Cassidy asked.

"Martin seems like a nice enough guy." A dreamy little smile feathered across Serena's lips. "Handsome too."

"He is handsome." Cassidy put her hands on her hips, anticipating what Serena might say next.

"But Lisa was acting all weird," she continued, her light smile turning into a faint frown.

"How so?"

"I don't know. She kept coming over and offering us more food and drinks. Maybe she has a crush on Martin or something. But that's just weird, cause she's old."

Lisa wasn't even thirty, but Cassidy kept her mouth shut.

"You think Lisa likes him?" Cassidy tried to keep the amusement from her voice.

"Yeah, and then when the interview was over, she asked if I'd taste something for her in the kitchen. It was one of those weird salt-and-vinegar sugar cookies. Totally not my thing."

"Hmm . . . I wonder what got into her?"

Thank you, Lisa. Her friend had done just what Cassidy asked of her.

"I don't know." She let out a breath and stretched out her arm, reaching for Cassidy's keys. "But now

I'm ready to sell some ice cream. Skye is going to fire me soon if I don't work for her more."

Cassidy remembered the financial troubles her friend was having. "I have a feeling she's fine not having an employee there right now. She's still trying to get back on her feet after the whole Buddy situation."

A competitor had opened across the street from her and wreaked havoc on Skye's business—and on her life. That was over now, but Skye was still recovering.

"I know." Serena frowned. "That was crazy. I'm kind of sad I wasn't here when it all happened. She could have used my support."

Serena would have only added to Skye's stress, most likely. But Cassidy didn't say that out loud.

"Okay, go sell some ice cream," Cassidy said, suddenly anxious to talk to the women staying in her house.

"It's so hot outside that I bet a lot of people are buying."

"You bet correctly," Cassidy said. "It's a good thing I got a new shipment in today."

As Serena left, Cassidy went upstairs to check on the women. She hoped and prayed they were doing okay.

Rose was sleeping soundly in her room when Cassidy came back, as was Kat.

Trina, however, was up and almost seemed to be waiting to talk to Cassidy.

"Trina, you're up and about," Cassidy said, grabbing a water bottle and taking a long sip.

"I'm doing much better. Thank you." Her voice sounded shaky.

Cassidy recognized a deep insecurity inside the woman. It wasn't one born of what had happened to her—though the abduction had most likely made things worse. No, Cassidy had seen this kind of emptiness before. It was an emptiness borne of a rough life, lacking a stable support system. Probably marred with abuse and people who'd let her down and the fact that no one had ever given her a soft place to fall.

Cassidy's heart panged at the realization.

"Can I fix you some tea?" Cassidy asked.

"I'd love some, if you wouldn't mind."

"Not at all. Hot or cold? I'm pretty proficient at both."

"Hot, please."

She went to the stove to prepare some. As she did, Trina sat at the breakfast bar and watched her.

"What's your story, Trina?" Cassidy asked, setting the kettle on the stove.

She stared at her hands a moment before shrugging.

"Bad home life. Shuffled to different foster-care families. Thought I met the perfect guy. Turns out he was a predator." She shrugged again. "Same old story, I guess."

"I'm sorry, Trina."

"I should have known better."

"What we all want deep inside is to trust someone, to know they're going to look out for our best interests." Cassidy swallowed hard at the words. That was true for her too, wasn't it? If only she could tell someone the truth . . .

She pulled out a mug and a tea bag and waited for the water to boil.

"I want the life I've always dreamed about. I thought Kent would give it to me."

"Is that what he called himself?"

"Yeah, I should have known that a guy like that would never be interested in me."

Cassidy squeezed her hand. "Don't sell yourself short."

"Look at me. I'm a mess. I had a drug problem and went into withdrawal when I was abducted. It was so bad . . . even right now, all I want is another hit. Makes me feel crazy sometimes."

"It's never too late to change."

Tears rimmed her eyes. "I have a daughter, you know."

Cassidy's heart pounded in her ears now, the sound cut by the squeal of the kettle. "Do you?"

"She's in foster care. I'm doing to her what I always blamed my mom for doing to me."

"We're going to get you out of this situation,

Trina." Cassidy poured the tea and slid the mug toward her. "You don't have to follow in your mother's footsteps."

"Why do you want to help us?"

"I . . . I don't believe in coincidences. I found you three for a reason."

"I was thinking the same thing, Cassidy." She offered a weak smile. "Anyone else would have run away or called the cops. You know you're putting yourself in danger by helping us."

"I believe in doing the right thing, even when it's hard."

"Thank you, Cassidy. May your kindness be repaid one day."

"You can repay me by staying clean."

She nodded a little too rapidly. "If get out of this, I will. I'm going to make some changes."

"I believe you, Trina. I believe you."

Chapter Eighteen

WHEN CASSIDY HAD A FREE MOMENT, she hopped on the computer.

Rose had mentioned that the Cobra said something about stopping in Myrtle Beach before coming here. Out of curiosity, she looked at the crime reports for the area.

She scanned each of them from the past three days, hoping something might make sense.

She finally found an article that did just that. Her heart pounded in her ears as she read the details.

A twenty-year-old was nearly abducted after trying to meet someone she'd first connected with on an internet dating site. The woman got a bad feeling in her gut and decided to cut the date short, but her online match didn't want to let her leave.

One of his friends even stepped in, and she'd thought for sure she would disappear never to be found. But before they could get her into their car, she pulled out a knife from her purse. She always kept it there as a precaution. She managed to slice one man's arm before getting away.

The Cobra.

Cassidy nibbled on her lip for a minute before making a decision. She put in an anonymous call to the Myrtle Beach Police Department, hinting that the man involved in this case may be in Lantern Beach, North Carolina, right now.

She didn't leave her name, and she stayed on the line for only a few minutes.

Then she hung up and prayed, hoping she hadn't done something she would regret.

She stepped outside, ready to get some fresh air and clear her head. She wandered downstairs where it was shady beneath her house. But as soon as her foot hit the pavement, she felt someone staring at her.

Renee.

She was pulling a bag from the back of her car.

"He's not yours," she said, crossing the distance between them.

"What are you talking about?" That had been abrupt.

Renee's eyes narrowed. "Ty and I need to see if we can work things out. That's never going to happen if you're around."

"I'm his neighbor. What do you want me to do?"

"Oh, I see the way he looks when he talks about you. Stay away from him."

"I really think that's Ty's choice, not yours." Cassidy felt herself bristling.

"He's already chosen."

"If that's true, he's all yours. I'm not about forcing someone to be with me."

A glimmer of a smile lit her gaze. "Good. Cause I'm not going anywhere. I already lost him once."

Renee stormed back upstairs, forgetting the suitcase she'd left behind her car.

Cassidy stood there a minute, the first touch of grief hitting her.

Had she really lost Ty before she ever really had him?

And, if so, why was that reality going to be harder to swallow than leaving Seattle behind had been?

An hour later, Cassidy stepped onto the deck.

She'd already fixed a large pot of chicken noodle soup for the ladies to eat later. As she'd worked, she'd wrestled with her thoughts. And now she felt a headache coming on.

Maybe some fresh air would help clear her mind.

This was the golden hour, her favorite time of the day. At an hour before sunset, the sky began to cast lovely colors across its expanse. The temperature was cooling off. Nighttime lingered close.

The ladies inside were fine. In fact, they seemed to

be doing great. They'd showered. Changed clothes. Eaten.

And now they were playing a game of Chinese checkers. They'd also binge-watched *Grey's Anatomy*, apparently. Everything felt calmer, and she was grateful for it.

But her quiet moment was interrupted by commotion next door.

Cassidy's head swung toward Ty's house just in time to see Renee storm onto the deck and slam the door behind her. Renee didn't stop either. She kept going down the stairs until she reached her car.

Even from the far distance, Cassidy could see the tears rolling down Renee's cheeks.

Uh-oh.

Maybe the woman had finally gotten the message that Ty wasn't interested.

And, even if Cassidy didn't particularly care for the woman, it was still agonizingly hard to see someone look so heartbroken.

She waited, listening as the car started. Pulled out. Squealed away.

She contemplated what to do next. But she knew inside exactly what she wanted to do.

Cassidy wanted to check on Ty and find out what had happened.

Before she could overthink anything, she trotted across the space between their houses and pounded on Ty's door. He opened it a few minutes later, a stormy expression on his face. His eyes softened ever so slightly when he saw Cassidy.

She soaked him in for a moment. His arm was in a sling, but his face was finally getting some color back. Overall, he looked 100 percent better.

"Cassidy. Come on in. But I've gotta warn you that I'm not in a great mood."

"I'm sorry to hear that." She stepped into his place, remembering the last time she'd been here. Remembering the jolt of panic she'd felt when she found Ty lying on the floor unresponsive.

"Can I get you something?" He paused and waited for Cassidy's response.

"Nope," she said. "I just came to check on you."

The corner of his lip pulled down in a frown. "You saw Renee leave?"

"Sure did." She glanced at the kitchen counter and saw the engagement ring there.

So she'd left it this time . . . interesting.

He sighed and sat down on the couch, a little harder than usual. Cassidy sat across from him and waited, giving him all the time he needed to formulate his thoughts. She could only guess the not-great mood was a direct result of the whole Renee situation.

"You know I tried to tell her how I was feeling, right?" he finally started.

"Right."

"And I was trying to be kind since she did come all the way out to Lantern Beach."

"I know."

"So she insisted on driving me home," Ty said. "I figured it couldn't hurt. Maybe once we were here we could sit down for a heart–to-heart, and I wasn't going to end the conversation until I was certain she understood that we were over."

"Okay." Cassidy tried not to show how anxious she was to hear where this story was going.

"After we got back, she started looking around the house. She found a picture of Kujo."

Cassidy swallowed hard, realizing this wasn't going to be good.

"She said she couldn't wait to meet him." Ty shook his head. "I don't know what happened, but I almost lost it. Not in a violent way, but in a brutally honest way. Unfortunately, that's what it took to get through to her."

"What did you say?"

"I guess I was holding onto to some repressed bitterness about the way she left things," he said. "I told her she wasn't getting anywhere near Kujo after the stunt she pulled with Ranger."

Every time Cassidy thought about how Renee had given his dog away to someone else while Ty was stationed overseas—without his permission—her blood boiled. And then Renee had picked up and left as well.

What kind of person did that?

It was all in very poor taste, especially considering how much Ty adored his canine friends.

"She looked all innocent, like she had no idea

what I was talking about," Ty continued. "She told me she'd loved Ranger and giving him away had broken her heart."

Uh-oh. This couldn't go anywhere good.

"I told her she could have left him with one of my friends. She could have told me what was going on."

"What did she say?"

"She said she was terribly confused and that her grief over missing me caused her to think and act in irrational ways. Then I asked her why she never returned any of my phone calls afterward. She said it was too hard."

It sounded like one difficult but very needed conversation. "I see."

"As we kept talking, it came out that she met someone else." Ty shook his head. "I figured that from the moment she showed up here. They broke up two weeks ago, and that made her realize how much she'd lost with me. She had a lot of nerve."

Cassidy couldn't argue with that. "She looked pretty upset."

"Well, I was the one who ended up apologizing before she left. I hate seeing women cry. I really hate being the one who makes them cry."

"But it sounded like you said things that needed to be said. Maybe you finally have some closure."

He nodded, but his shoulders still looked hunched and burdened. "I guess so. I just feel like the bad guy right now, and I'm not sure why. It's a horrible feeling."

"That's your compassion speaking. It's not a bad thing to feel horrible after breaking someone's heart."

His gaze met hers, and Cassidy could see the gratitude there.

"I'm glad you came by." He shifted and rolled his good shoulder back. "Listen, can you stick around for a few minutes? I need to hop in the shower, but I'm not ready for you to leave yet."

"You're not ready for me to?" Her tone was inquisitive and teasing.

He shrugged. "I've missed hanging out with you. Just . . . stay, okay? I won't be long."

She smiled, secretly delighted to spend more time with him. "Sure thing."

Mac stopped by to drop off Kujo while Ty was in the shower. Which worked out perfectly since Cassidy had some questions for him.

Right after she gave Kujo a little bit of loving, of course.

"Did you look into Smith Anderson?" She'd called Mac earlier and asked him to do some research. His connections in town were far greater than hers.

"I did talk to a few people. I found out some things that you'll find very interesting, I think."

"Please share."

"You were right, he is trying to bypass some town

statutes and build a hotel here. He has a plan all worked out."

"Is he using drug money to fund it?"

A knot formed between Mac's eyes. "Drug money? No, it's a well-known fact that his family is loaded. I'm sure he hasn't had any trouble getting the funding."

Okay, so there went that theory. "Well, do you know when he got into town?"

"As a matter of fact, I do." He crossed his arms and propped his hip against the counter. "He arrived two days ago on his first vacation in six years."

"First vacation in six years?" That couldn't be right.

"He's been on the news five nights a week for the past six years."

That was quite the alibi. He probably hadn't had time to travel to an island and oversee a human trafficking operation.

"Is he working with Niles, by chance, to get this hotel approved?"

Mac's eyes morphed from matter-of-fact to impressed. "How'd you know?"

"Lucky guess."

He gave her a look. "Care to explain your line of reasoning?"

Cassidy scrambled for an excuse and finally settled on, "Just some things I overheard while I was on my route. You know me and my curiosity."

The look in his eyes told her he didn't buy the

excuse. "I have a feeling you're tapping into that hidden talent you have for nosing out trouble. Just be careful. People don't take kindly to people digging into their business."

Didn't she know. Didn't she ever know.

Chapter Nineteen

CASSIDY SUCKED in a breath when Ty emerged from the bathroom ten minutes later. His hair glistened, and his skin looked clean and dewy. Plus, the scent of some kind of spicy shampoo surrounded him.

Kujo took off down the hallway toward him. Cassidy smiled as she watched their reunion. Ty looked as happy to see his dog as the dog did to see him.

"Mac stopped by, I see?" Ty said.

"He sure did."

"I feel a little better now." He stepped toward her and ran his hand down his freshly shaven jaw. "Thanks for waiting."

Her throat suddenly felt tight, and she had to look away. She nodded toward the kitchen instead. "It's no problem. Do you want me to fix you something to eat?"

"You'd do that?"

Cassidy quickly moved herself into the kitchen, separating herself from Ty with the breakfast bar counter. "Though the thought of watching you go hungry is so tempting, I suppose I could manage to scrounge you up something."

Humor. She hadn't realized how great it was when it came to diversion tactics until she arrived on the island. Now that she was away from everyone's expectations of her, she seemed to be discovering who she really was.

Ty smiled and propped his hip against the counter. "And there's that sarcasm I've missed so much."

Funny, Cassidy had never been especially sarcastic before she came here. But now she found herself teasing and laughing and enjoying quiet time. Had it taken her life being completely shaken to realize the person who'd been buried deep down inside her?

"What would you like?" she asked, feeling unwelcome emotions rising up inside. Undeniable attraction. Longing for more than friendship. A hunger for something deeper than life as she'd known it.

"I've been dying for something other than the food at the clinic." Ty walked past her and pulled out a stainless-steel pan. "Do you know how to make tuna?"

"It's easy. You just open the top of the can and—"

He tilted his head, his eyes sparkling. "Fresh tuna. Tuna steak?"

She shrugged and edged away from him. "No idea. But I'm a fast learner. Look how quickly I learned to be the ice cream lady."

He smiled. "Amazingly fast. Now, how about if I help you make dinner—with one arm?"

"Don't you need to rest?" Distance would be good right now, even though her heart might disagree.

"I think I'll be okay supervising in the kitchen." He opened the fridge and pulled out something wrapped in white paper. "Austin dropped these by earlier. Are you hungry too?"

"I could probably eat."

Cassidy's mind went back to the women at her house. They'd be okay there for a little while. She'd left them food. They were tired, and just seemed to want to relax, to recover, to gain their strength for whatever happened next. And there was nothing else Cassidy could do for them tonight. And Ty could use a hand . . .

He directed her on what oil to use, how to season the tuna, and when to put it into the pan. Cassidy totally felt like she was in over her head. Or maybe it was just Ty that was making her feel this way because suddenly she felt jittery and self-conscious. Especially when Ty ended up behind her with one arm snaked around her waist as he helped her manage everything on the stove.

It would be so easy to just turn around and . . .

Her breath caught.

No, Cassidy couldn't let herself think like that.

Starting a relationship with Ty would just be complicated. Too complicated. And when he discovered who she was . . . that she'd been lying to him . . . that she wasn't who she claimed . . . she had no idea how he would react.

She managed to cook the rest of the meal without incident.

When they sat down to eat, Cassidy had some questions begging to be asked. Conversations needing to be had. She'd never been one to believe in putting off the inevitable.

She laid her fork back on her plate and cleared her throat. "Ty, I wish you'd told me about your surgery. I know we started to talk about this at the clinic, but I could tell you were exhausted. You told me that you had to take care of some things for Hope House."

He frowned, lowering his fork also. "I was, in a way. I knew I needed this surgery before I could continue making plans. I'd be no good to anyone if I couldn't use my shoulder like I needed to. I'd been delaying the inevitable."

"But it was more than that," she prodded, not letting him off the hook that easily. "This was a big deal, and you closed me—I mean, your friends—you closed me and your other friends out."

That had been a slip. There was nothing between them—just because they'd kissed didn't mean she deserved any special treatment.

Ty shrugged, and his gaze latched onto hers. "I

suppose I didn't want to swallow my pride, Cassidy. No guy wants to think of himself as weak."

"Surgery would make you weak?"

He let out a sigh and looked out the window a moment, as if gathering his thoughts. "I guess I'm a better warrior than I am patient."

"That's no surprise." It wasn't. He was trained to keep going, to complete the mission, to not let anything stop him.

She got that. Yet there were times when a person had to ask for help. The key was knowing when.

Cassidy supposed that advice could be applied to herself, as well.

"I thought I'd just get the surgery out of the way, spend a little time in rehab, and come back to resume life here as if nothing had happened."

She raised an eyebrow and began eating again. "That sounds awfully optimistic of you."

"True, and strange because I'm not usually an optimist. And, if anything, this further proves that I should not become one."

"I'm glad I found you when I did." Cassidy's throat tightened at her words. What if she hadn't? What if . . . No, she couldn't let herself go there.

"I know." He reached across the table and squeezed her hand. "Believe me, I know."

If she hadn't, things would be different right now. And Cassidy would have lost a man who was perhaps the best person she'd ever know.

After dinner, Ty had started a fire that warmed them. It wasn't particularly cold outside, but the nights did have a slight chill to them. Kujo lay near the crackling blaze. The smell of sautéed vegetables still lingered in the air. And the night outside the windows was inky and alluring.

Then he excused himself to the couch. The way he cringed and rolled his shoulder made it clear he wasn't comfortable. "Since the surgery, my muscles have been unbearably tight."

Cassidy watched as he struggled to reach his back and rub out the kinks.

She hesitated a moment, contemplating the wisdom of her choices. Then she sighed and stood from her chair.

"I can't watch this anymore," she said. "Scoot up."

"What?" His eyebrows knit together in confusion.

"You heard me," she said. "Scoot up. I'll rub your back for you."

"I wasn't hinting." His hand dropped back into his lap. "I promise."

She didn't believe him, and she quirked an eyebrow to let him know. "Don't make me rescind my offer."

His eyes glimmered with amusement. "Fine then. If you insist."

Oh, sure. She was insisting.

She sat behind Ty on the couch and started working the muscles on his good shoulder. They were incredibly tight. And incredibly impressive.

Not that she noticed.

Except she did.

"You're pretty good at this," he said, his muscles relaxing beneath her fingers.

"Yeah, well, I did play soft—" Cassidy stopped cold. She'd been about to say *softball*. What was she thinking? That was her old life. Not her right now life.

"You played what?"

Cassidy swallowed hard but massaged even harder, hoping to distract him. It didn't work. Ty didn't complain or flinch once.

It couldn't hurt to tell Ty that she'd been a softball player once upon a time. He wouldn't be able to connect that detail with her old life back in Seattle. Of all the things about herself that Cassidy needed to keep a secret, her athleticism wasn't at the top of her list.

"I used to play softball." Despite Cassidy's reasoning only seconds ago, her throat tightened as she said the words, as if her body knew she was entering dangerous territory.

"Did you just share something about your past? I like this." The amusement remained in his voice, but this time it mingled with a touch of sincerity.

Another wave of apprehension swept over Cassidy. She feared making that one fatal mistake—

the one she couldn't make right and that proved she was a fraud.

Now more than ever it felt entirely too important that she keep up her carefully crafted identity. "I did."

"Oh, yeah. Were you any good at the sport?"

"I like to think so." Cassidy had been offered scholarships to play in college, but she'd rejected those offers, as well as her father's encouragement that she go to business school. Instead, she'd become a police officer.

"I like hearing about you, Cassidy." Ty's voice sounded as smooth as butter—butter mixed with sugar.

A sad smile pulled at Cassidy's lips. If only she could tell him the truth. If she could tell someone. Anyone. Silence was an isolation lonelier than a deserted island.

Her competing desires played a fierce game of tug-of-war inside her.

Instead, Cassidy concentrated on continuing to work Ty's muscles and enjoying the quiet of the house.

"You've got a gift," Ty muttered, rolling his neck. "Thank you for sharing."

"Anytime." Well, not anytime. That had just slipped out.

"I'll keep that in mind." His voice curled with satisfaction.

Of course Ty wouldn't let that go. Cassidy ended

her little therapy session with a friendly pat on the back. "Hopefully, that helps some."

"Oh, it does."

Before she could stand and put the proper distance between herself and Ty, he leaned back. Somehow, he managed to reach around her, grab her arm, and slide it around his chest.

"Smooth move," she muttered with a laugh.

"It was, wasn't it?" Ty settled back, resting his head and back against her.

The smell of his leathery aftershave, mixed with the spicy aura of his shampoo, filled her senses. Made her close her eyes and inhale long, deep breaths.

This should feel weird. But it didn't.

"Please tell me how this is going to help your shoulder," she said, ignoring the unmistakable pleasure that filled her.

"It helps me relax." He paused and let out a contented sigh. "You smell good."

"Do I?" Surprising delight rippled through her, but she quickly snapped from her stupor. *Get a handle on your emotions, Cassidy.* "Well, I'm going to hurt your shoulder."

"Nah. Just don't touch it."

It was kind of hard not to touch it when he was leaning against her. He was so relaxed that it seemed as if they'd done this before. They hadn't.

Ty let out another contented sigh. "This is perfect."

"What's perfect?" Cassidy needed clarification, just for her own sanity.

"The quiet. Being out of the clinic. Kujo. You and me."

Her throat went dry. *You and me?* There shouldn't be any Cassidy and Ty. Yet why did it feel like life kept drawing them together?

Cassidy wanted to argue. She *should* argue.

But she didn't.

Instead, her fingers tightened against Ty's chest. His defined chest. She decided to just enjoy the moment as well and melted into him.

If only every minute could feel this right. This perfect.

Within a few minutes, Ty was asleep.

Cassidy waited, watching him rest. Resisting the urge to trace the lines of his face. To touch his hair.

When she was sure he was slumbering, she slipped out from beneath him, leaned down, and kissed his temple. "Good night, Ty."

Then she disappeared outside, wondering exactly what she was doing.

Cassidy stuffed her hands in the pockets of her jean shorts as she slowly wandered from Ty's place. That had felt a little too much like home. Like something she wanted to do forever.

Her heart physically ached at the realization that

she'd have to leave here one day. Why had one of the hardest decisions of her life led to possibly some of the best choices for her future?

As her feet hit the sandy path between Ty's place and hers, a pop echoed in the distance.

Cassidy froze. What was that sound?

After a moment of contemplation, she started toward that small patch of woods that separated her place from the streets beyond it.

Her gut told her that noise was no coincidence. That it wasn't an out-of-towner experimenting early with fireworks—although she'd been told to expect plenty of that. That sounded like gunfire.

She slipped back into the thick underbrush of the maritime woods, ignoring the shiver that ran down her spine. Something about forests had always scared her. But these woods in particular were thick with low-lying branches of trees that caused her to walk with a hunched back.

Yesterday, she'd been in a hurry as she rushed through them. Today, she had too much time to contemplate as she wandered.

Finally, she reached the clearing on the other side and paused.

Just as she suspected, that noise had come from the house where the ladies had been staying.

And, right now, a black sedan was parked in the driveway.

Someone was looking for those ladies, she realized. Whoever it was probably thought he'd found them. How much longer before someone discovered they were staying with Cassidy? She couldn't deny it was a possibility.

She nibbled on her bottom lip as she contemplated her choices.

This was her chance to figure out who these guys might be. If she knew and could get the police to arrest them, then maybe these women would have a chance at freedom.

But Cassidy needed to watch her back or things would turn ugly. She had no backup out here.

She crept closer to the house, moving along the perimeter of the trees.

Another crash sounded inside the house.

Whoever was in there was mad. Upset.

They must have gotten a tip that the women were there and come back only to discover them gone.

Cassidy closed her eyes a minute, grateful she'd found the ladies when she had. Otherwise . . . she couldn't bear to think about it.

Wait here, she told herself. Watch and wait.

It was the best—and safest—thing she could do.

Good things come to those who wait.

All Cassidy needed was a face. A clue about who was behind this. And she could take it from there.

As she drew in a deep breath, the crickets around her went quiet.

A branch cracked.

Before Cassidy could turn around, something slammed into her head.

Chapter Twenty

CASSIDY BLINKED AWAY the pain and swung around. As she did, something collided with the side of her head.

Again.

A fist.

Her world spun but only momentarily.

She straightened, and her gaze cleared. A masked man hunched in front of her, his body ready for combat.

As he swung at her again, she ducked. His fist collided with the tree behind her. He muttered a curse before growling and lunging again.

Cassidy braced herself for his attack. Her shoulder collided with his abdomen. The man gasped as she used his momentum to hurl him over her shoulder.

She swung around and saw him roll to his feet.

He was spry. She'd give him that.

The grunting sounds the man made left no mistakes that he was angry now.

Before she could catch her breath, he lunged at Cassidy again. His body collided with hers, and she hit the ground hard.

Jerking her hands above her head, he pinned her against the prickly grass with the ease of someone who'd done this many times before. He panted, staring at her with angry eyes.

Cassidy moaned as the air left her lungs.

"Who are you?" he growled, his weight crushing her.

She cringed, trying not to show her pain. "Who are you?"

"I should kill you right now."

The moisture left Cassidy's throat. If only she'd had time to grab her gun. Or if she'd told someone what she was doing. It was too late for any of that.

"I heard a noise," she said, softening her voice to a plea. *Low profile and laid-back beach girl.* She kept forgetting. "I was checking it out."

The man lifted Cassidy just high enough that it hurt when he rammed her back down into the ground. "Who are you, really?"

She moaned, her teeth clenched. "I told you. I thought I heard some fireworks. My boyfriend gets freaked out when he hears them. He's a vet. Iraqi war."

He paused, as if contemplating her words.

"Let's go!" someone yelled in the distance.

"Stay away," the man warned, turning back to Cassidy. "And forget you ever saw me."

Cassidy said nothing.

Suddenly his gaze changed, as if he had a new thought. "Or maybe I should bring you with me. You're a pretty little thing. We could get good money for you."

Cassidy's pulse pounded so hard she feared it would burst from her chest. Before she could say anything, the man pulled himself off her and grabbed her arm. He began dragging her toward the car.

No. If she got in that car, her chances of getting away—or even surviving—would be close to zero.

"What are you doing?" the other masked man said.

"Look who I found snooping around. We could get top dollar for a blonde like this."

"Please, I just thought I heard fireworks and my boyfriend is freaking out," Cassidy said, making sure to use all her panic as a smoke screen. "He has PTSD. Let me go. I won't say anything."

"You shouldn't have been snooping," the other man—the burlier of the two—said. "But it's too risky to take her."

"What are we going to do with her then?"

Cassidy licked her lips as she waited, anticipated, formulated.

"We can't let her go now, can we?" Burly Guy said. "You already shot off your gun, mistaking a rat for a person. It's a wonder the police aren't here yet."

"That was the biggest rat I've ever seen."

"Please, I haven't even seen your faces," Cassidy said. "I know nothing."

"The boss would like her, though, wouldn't he?" The man squeezed her arm harder.

"Maybe he'd forgive us for what happened with the other three." Burly Guy seemed to be contemplating his options now.

Cassidy's heart continued to pound. She might be able to take one of these guys. But both of them? It was unlikely. She was winded and unarmed. Both men were easily stronger than her.

"Put her in the trunk," Burly Guy said.

Oh no. Cassidy couldn't let this happen.

She let out a blood-curdling scream and began thrashing against the man's grasp. If, for nothing else, maybe she could alert someone else. Because she'd be no good to anyone if these guys took her.

The man who'd grabbed her wrapped his arms around her midsection and lifted her. "Shut up!"

No way would Cassidy do that.

Using ever bit of her survival instinct, she kicked him—where it hurt.

His grip on her loosened as he bent over in pain.

Wasting no time, Cassidy took off down the street.

Burly Guy lunged at her and caught her ankles.

She hit the gravel lane with a thud. Her entire body ached on impact, and she could feel the skin ripping at her elbows.

"What do you think you're doing?" the man growled again. "Not so fast."

She flipped over and kicked, this time hitting the man in the nose.

He groaned with pain.

The action had pulled at his mask. She saw the glimpse of a face.

Square jaw. Dark hair.

No, Cassidy didn't recognize him. But at least she had something now.

She scrambled to her feet.

She couldn't run back to the woods, couldn't lead the men to her place.

Instead Cassidy cut through the yards around her.

But pain sliced through her leg, slowing her down.

Grass swished around her. Branches broke.

They were after her. And getting closer by the moment.

Cassidy wasn't sure how much farther she'd make it before they caught her.

She needed to think of a Plan B.

Come on, Cassidy. Think! You know this area just as well as any local.

An idea hit her, something she'd seen on one of her routes.

It was risky. But it just might work.

She cut one more street over and saw the house she'd been looking for. She ran around it, trying to lose the men. To buy herself enough time.

As soon as she rounded the corner, she did a U-turn and headed toward the oceanside pool located next to the property.

Erosion had pulled away the sand from beneath the pool. She noted it every time she drove past. But in the dark, it wasn't noticeable.

And it might just be her best place to hide.

Before she could overthink it, she darted into the space and wedged herself between the prefabricated pool and the sand.

And then she waited.

As she heard the footsteps approaching, she held her breath.

Had they seen her? Would they find her? And, if they did, did Cassidy have the strength to fight them?

She wasn't sure.

Chapter Twenty-One

"WHERE'D SHE GO?" one of the men muttered.

Cassidy pulled her arms and legs closer, hoping the darkness concealed her. The sand beneath her offered a cushioned hiding spot, but a sand crab only two feet away stared at her, silently warning that Cassidy was in his territory now. As she stared back at the creature, she shivered.

He was right. This wasn't her territory. But she'd make the best of it. At least the roar of the ocean concealed any telltale sounds she might make.

"I don't know where she went," Spry Man said. "She couldn't have gotten away that fast."

Cassidy could see their feet in the distance. They'd paused near the edge of the lane but were close enough that she could make out their words.

"She's collateral damage at this point," Burly Guy said. "She saw my face when she kicked my mask off."

"Maybe she won't say anything."

"Did you see her eyes?" Burly Guy's voice rose with emotion. "The girl's got spunk. I doubt she's going to let this go."

"What are we supposed to do?"

"Find her." Burly Guy began pacing.

"Well, she's gone. I don't know how we're supposed to do that."

"Then we keep looking. Tomorrow and the next day until we eliminate this problem. If the Cobra finds out about this . . . he'll kill us. He'll do to us what he did to Larson. And you know it's true. He can't handle mistakes."

Spry began muttering obscenities beneath his breath. "This was her mistake, not ours. She shouldn't have been snooping around."

"You think she knows where the women are?" The two men walked closer to the pool.

Cassidy froze, praying the shadows and darkness concealed her.

"Nah, you heard her. She thought her boyfriend might flip out because of fireworks."

"She must live close by."

No, no, no! That was the last thing Cassidy wanted them to realize.

"So we'll keep our eyes open then," Spry said. "We'll find her. It's just a matter of time."

The footsteps faded.

Cassidy drew in a deep breath. She could hear her mental clock ticking. The men were right. It was just a matter of time until they figured out who she was.

Cassidy waited, needing to be certain the men were gone. She couldn't call the police. Not only did she have no faith in the local PD, but they might ask too many questions. It was better if she handled this herself.

She stared at the crab still, the crab that silently challenged her. She wished she had a hole to climb into and disappear just like the little crustacean did, but that didn't seem possible for her life.

She shifted slightly. Her elbows hurt from her fall. Her head ached from where she'd hit the ground. Her knees were skinned and covered with sand.

None of those things began to measure up to what Rose, Kat, and Trina had been through, though.

Twenty minutes later, Cassidy emerged. As soon as she climbed out, she nearly collapsed.

She must have hit her head harder than she thought.

She rubbed her neck and glanced around. She didn't see anything or anyone.

As her gaze wandered down the lane, she realized she'd run farther than she thought.

Probably a mile.

Cassidy wasn't sure she could make it back home without collapsing.

After a moment of contemplation, she pulled out her phone and stared at it.

She had people she could call, but she didn't want to call any of them. They'd ask too many questions. Her request would arouse too many suspicions.

There was a chance these guys would find her if she walked down the road. Or she could pass out. The distance felt insurmountable at the moment.

Pride comes before a fall.

She remembered what happened when Ty hadn't swallowed his pride. He'd almost died as a result.

Did Cassidy want to do that also? She wouldn't be a lot of good to anyone dead . . . or in the hospital. And in the hospital, they'd want her insurance information. Her name. Her background.

All things that could point the way for the wrong people.

With that in mind, Cassidy dialed Ty's number . . . and prayed she wasn't making a mistake.

Chapter Twenty-Two

TY JERKED from his slumber at the sound of his cell phone singing "Anchor's Away." Renee had programmed that for him, against his wishes. Wait . . . he was sleeping on the couch?

The memory of Cassidy being here hit him, and he jetted upright, scanning the room.

He was alone. Cassidy must have gone home.

As the song continued, he grabbed his phone from the table.

Cassidy's number appeared on the screen. Why was she calling him at . . . he checked the time . . . 1:30 in the morning?

He quickly answered, knowing that something must be wrong.

"Ty, I need your help." Her voice sounded hushed and breathless. "Could you . . . could you pick me up?"

"What's wrong?" Alarm panged through him.

She'd just been here. What had happened in the brief amount of time since she'd left?

"I'll explain later. Please. I'm on Sand Piper Drive. I can meet you at the end of the lane. Near the sand dune. Flash your lights, okay?"

He didn't like the sound of this. But it wasn't the time to ask questions. He'd do that later. "I'll be right there."

He jetted from the couch and grabbed his keys. Thankfully he hadn't taken his pain medicine, so he should be fine to drive. He climbed in his truck and hurried from his driveway, down the gravel lane, and to the highway.

Slow is fast, he reminded himself. Foolish mistakes happened when people acted too quickly or impulsively, so he made sure to pace himself. Finally, he spotted Sand Piper Drive.

As he approached the end of the lane, he flashed his lights, just as he'd told Cassidy he would. But he saw no one out here—only dark beach houses and shadowed sand dunes and a kayak that had been left near a rickety fence.

Suddenly, someone darted from behind one of the houses.

Cassidy.

She scrambled into his truck, her breathing labored as she slammed the door.

Ty's heart thudded into his chest when he saw her. Blood trickled from her forehead. Her eye was turning black. She limped.

He reached for her, concern solidifying in his gut. She was in trouble. "Cassidy . . ."

"We need to go," she whispered. "Please."

He didn't argue. He heard the desperation in her voice and backed out of the lane.

Cassidy glanced behind them as they started back to his place.

Who was she looking for? Who had done this to her?

He restrained himself from asking the questions— even though he desperately wanted to. Anger burned him up at the thought of anyone hurting her. But he'd give her the space she requested. For now.

He couldn't reach his place soon enough. As soon as he pulled in, he quickly parked his truck and hurried from the driver's side. At the other side of the vehicle, Cassidy had already climbed out, but the list-lessness in her movements caused another shot of concern to rush through him.

With his uninjured arm, he slipped a hand around Cassidy's waist to help support her and started toward her house.

She froze on his driveway. "Can we go to your place?"

"I guess. I mean, sure. I just thought . . ."

Her face looked unusually pale as she licked her lips and shifted uncomfortably. "Long story."

Cassidy had a lot of those.

Ty helped her upstairs, not letting her go until he'd deposited her on his couch.

"Let me get the first aid kit." Ty reappeared a few minutes later with the plastic box and squeezed some ointment on a cotton ball. He cringed when he saw her elbows. "We're going to have to rinse the sand from those wounds first."

Her eyelids sank but she nodded. He led her to the sink and held her cuts beneath water he'd let warm for a minute. After patting her elbows dry with a paper towel, he sat her back down and dabbed the cut on her forehead, then her elbows and knees. He put Band-Aids over each. Then he grabbed some frozen corn from the freezer for her to place on her eye.

Once all the necessities were taken care of, he waited.

To his surprise, Cassidy didn't say anything. Instead, she curled into him, her mind seeming a million miles away.

He wrapped his arm around her and pulled her close, tucking her head under his chin. Slowly, her breathing evened out and her heart *thump, thumping* against him seemed to slow. She smelled like salty air, and her limbs were covered with sand, but he didn't care. He was just happy she was okay.

"Do you want to talk about it?" he murmured, her hair tickling his chin.

"Not really."

His muscles began to tighten uncomfortably again. "Maybe we should call the police."

She stiffened. "No. Definitely not."

"Whoever did this to you needs to pay." Because

this hadn't happened by accident. No, someone had hurt Cassidy. That wasn't okay.

"The police will only make things worse."

"How so?" She wasn't making any sense.

"I promised not to tell."

His breath caught. "Who did you promise? What aren't you telling me, Cassidy?"

"I can't say."

"You're not making any sense." He was tired of being left in the dark.

"I know." She raised her head and rubbed her temples.

"Can you please tell me what's going on, Cassidy? Let me in."

She turned toward him, her big eyes full of apology and regret. "Let's just say I was in the wrong place at the wrong time. These men thought I was spying on them, but I wasn't. Then they tried to abduct me."

His stomach clenched tighter. He didn't like the sound of this. "Cassidy . . . I'm sorry."

She said nothing, only continued to rub her temples.

There was still something that didn't make sense. . . "But I don't understand what that has to do with a promise of any sort. You were in the wrong place, at the wrong time."

She glanced at him again, pleading with her eyes. But there was something else in her gaze as well. Was that determination? Anger? Ty wasn't sure.

"They said they're going to find me, Ty. If you call the police, they'll know. They're watching."

"Who were these guys?" He needed more.

Cassidy slowly swung her head back and forth. "I'm not sure, but they're up to no good. They said they'd take me back to their boss. That he would like me." Her voice cracked.

Anger flared up and down Ty's spine as he pictured the what-ifs and what-could-have-beens. Cassidy had come dangerously close to disappearing, and he could hardly swallow the thought.

"I don't like the sound of that. Could you just start at the beginning?"

Cassidy pulled away from him, and Ty instantly missed her closeness. But he gave her the space she needed—that she'd silently asked for. She ran a hand through her hair and removed the frozen corn from the side of her face.

"After you fell asleep, I left and started back to my place. But I heard something the next street over. A pop. So I went to make sure everything was okay."

"Without calling me first?"

She shrugged. "You were sleeping really well, and I figured it was just fireworks."

"It doesn't matter. You could have woken me."

"But I didn't think it was a big deal. Not really."

Ty wasn't sure if he believed that. If it hadn't been a big deal, she wouldn't have checked it out. But he let her continue.

"So I went to make sure everything was okay, and

these two men appeared. They started threatening me. I managed to get away—to hide. It was dumb luck. But . . . for a while there, I wasn't sure it was going to work."

Ty pulled Cassidy back toward him and wrapped his arm around her. Part of him wished he never had to let her go, that he could keep her safe forever. "Cassidy . . ."

"I knew if they took me, I would to be a goner. No one would ever see me again."

There was that thought again—the one he couldn't stomach. Instead he turned his thoughts to the tangible. "Were these men you saw doing something illegal?"

"I . . . I don't know. I couldn't tell. But they were acting suspiciously. Wearing all black. And masks."

Ty knew there was more to Cassidy's story. He'd found a stash of guns hidden at her place. He hadn't told her that yet. But he hadn't forgotten either.

"I should go," she muttered, starting to stand.

Ty caught her arm and tugged her back down beside him on the couch. "Cassidy . . ."

He had so much he wanted to ask her. But he wanted Cassidy to trust him enough to open up. He didn't want to have to pull the information from her.

As Cassidy's gaze caught his, Ty felt all his defenses weakening. She did something to him that he couldn't remember anyone else ever doing.

"Renee was a fool to leave you," Cassidy whispered.

The fear was gone from her eyes, along with the anger. The secrets. Instead, he saw . . . love? Was that what it was?

"I just want you to know that," she finished.

His defenses crumbled even more. Ty cupped his hand on the side of her face, wanting to forget his promise—his promise that he'd honor Cassidy's request and give her time. Cassidy's eyes were like whirlpools that pulled him under every time.

"Cassidy . . ." he whispered.

He closed his eyes and implored every ounce of his strength. Because everything he wanted was in front of him right now.

Chapter Twenty-Three

CASSIDY WASN'T sure what she was doing. She only knew that, at this moment, Ty meant everything in the world to her.

Renee showing up here had solidified her feelings for the man, as had the thought of losing him.

And even though she knew she should resist, Ty Chambers seemed too good to pass up.

Before she could second-guess herself, she reached up and pressed her lips against his.

The next instant, Ty swept her toward him, and his lips ravished hers. Maybe it was the knock on the head that had done it to her. Or the thought of Ty being with someone else. Or the tenderness by which he'd tended to her wounds.

Or maybe she'd just lost all her common sense. That was the most likely conclusion.

Cassidy only knew she never wanted to let Ty Chambers go.

And that thought was both thrilling and terrifying.

Cassidy pulled away from him and sucked in some deep breaths, lowering her head so Ty couldn't see her eyes. Beneath her fingers, she could feel his heart pounding just as rapidly as her own.

You're going to leave him one day, just like Renee did. Without explanation.

The thought slammed into her head so fast and hard that it jarred her.

Cassidy wanted to deny it. But she couldn't.

Because that was the truth. When everything played out, she was going to break his heart in the end. This situation was no win for both of them, and she'd be wise to keep that in mind.

"I shouldn't have done that," she whispered, staring at his chest—at anything but his lips.

Ty leaned closer—close enough that his breath tickled her cheek. "I would have to disagree with you."

His voice sounded intimate and low and sent another round of shivers up Cassidy's spine.

She sucked in a breath, reaching up to stroke his cheek and stare into the gaze she'd come to love. That was her second mistake. Because the warm brown eyes that stared back at her melted her heart . . . and nearly her resolve.

"I need to go." Cassidy's voice cracked with emotion.

Ty gripped her arm, keeping her in place. "Do you need to go? Or are you running away?"

What she wouldn't give to tell him the truth—about everything. But she couldn't. And that was a big burden to carry.

"I don't know. Both."

He tilted his head. "You're killing me, Cassidy."

"That's the last thing I want to do." She slid her hand from his jaw to the back of his neck. Everything in her urged her to let go. To leave. Yet she couldn't seem to obey.

"I wish you'd talk to me," he whispered.

"I should go."

When she looked into his eyes again, she saw the heat there. The attraction. The longing.

He cleared his throat. "You probably should. I can walk you back."

She quickly shook her head, feeling the urgent need to get away from him before she did something she regretted. "No . . . no. I mean, I'll be fine. It's better if you stay."

On more than one level.

Ty ran a hand through his hair, leaving it messier than usual. "I'll watch you go back then."

"That's . . . good. Perfect, actually. You can just watch." Move your hands away from his neck, Cassidy told herself.

Yet she found herself arching forward, just as Ty dipped down. Their lips met again, just as explosive this time as last.

She could kiss him like this . . . forever. Yet those thoughts made her lose touch with reality.

Bad idea.

They finally pulled away, and it was like a sonic boom sounded in the room.

"I should go," she said again, her voice hoarse with emotion.

This time, Ty didn't argue.

"What happened to you?" Rose rushed to meet Cassidy as soon as she walked in the door to her house. "Your eye is black, you're bandaged up and . . . even your lips are swollen."

Cassidy's hand went to her mouth, and she felt her cheeks redden. Well. . . how would she explain that? Easy—she wouldn't.

"I'm fine." Cassidy closed the door and locked it behind her, surprised to see all the women were awake still. It was nearly morning. "I just had a little run-in with the men who abducted you."

All three women gathered around her, and Cassidy told them what happened. Most of it, at least. She left out the part about the kiss.

"What are we going to do?" Rose paced the living room. "They're going to find us."

"They don't know who I am or where I live," Cassidy told them, perching herself in an armchair. The physical and emotional exhaustion she felt at the moment overwhelmed her. "So you'll be good for a while longer. I've been trying to figure out who these guys are."

"I'm glad you're okay." Kat sat on a stool at the kitchen counter and pulled her sweatshirt sleeves over her hands.

"Thank you. You didn't have to wait up. I'm sorry to make you all worry."

"We thought they killed you." Trina's voice trembled. She leaned against the wall with her arms drawn over her chest. She wore one of Cassidy's tank tops and a flowy skirt that looked huge on her skeletal frame.

"No, but they were scary." Cassidy pulled out her phone and typed in a few things on her Internet browser. "Do you recognize either of these men?"

First, she showed them the picture of Martin Chaser. Next, she showed them Smith Anderson.

None of the women showed any recognition to either man.

Rose's jaw flexed as her eyes narrowed. "Do you think one of these men is responsible?"

"I'm not sure," Cassidy admitted. "The island isn't that large, but it is full of tourists. So it's a matter of sorting through them."

"Thank you for everything you've done for us," Trina said.

"I wish I could do more." Cassidy released a long breath, hating feeling like she was powerless. "I'm going to keep digging. There's someone I know who might be able to help me. But I'd need to tell him what's going on."

"What?" Rose stood, fire flaring to life in her eyes. "No. You can't. You promised."

Cassidy raised her hands in the air, hoping for some peace before emotions got out of control. "And I won't—not without your permission. I'm just saying this is a lot to do on my own."

Rose stared at her, cynicism in her cool gaze. "How do you know you can trust this other person?"

"Because he's helped me before. He has a lot of connections. The thing is, time isn't on our side at this point. And me doing this alone . . . it's slow. I need help. You all need help."

The women looked at each other, and Cassidy could sense they needed to talk.

"How about this?" Cassidy stood and softened her voice, knowing better than to try and back them into a corner. "Don't give me an answer yet. But think about it overnight and let me know. I know you all want answers, even more than I do."

"We'll think about it," Rose promised, her voice as pinched as her expression.

"Good," Cassidy said. "And now I've got to get to bed. I'll talk to you all in the morning."

But it looked like she was back to square one. Smith Anderson was out, as well as Martin Chaser.

There was always Niles Shepherd. Maybe. She wasn't convinced he had motive, means, or opportunity.

But Cassidy knew these ladies couldn't stay here indefinitely. They needed help—physically, emotionally, and maybe even spiritually.

Chapter Twenty-Four

14 WEEKS EARLIER

"HELP US," one of the women whispered. "Please."

Dear Lord. What in the world . . .

These women were being held prisoners. The scent of body odor and urine rose up around Cady, indicating there were no facilities. Had these women even eaten?

Cady's heart pounded so rapidly she feared she might pass out. She had to do something. But what could she do that wouldn't blow her whole cover?

She wasn't sure, but she couldn't turn a blind eye to this.

One of the women stared up at her, a gag in her mouth and fear etched into her eyes. Her blonde hair was stringy around her face—greasy, as if she hadn't showered for weeks. She wore a white shirt that was stained with sweat and droplets of blood, along with some jeans.

Cady squatted down. "I'm going to help you," she whispered.

She grabbed a small rod she'd used to pick the outside lock and worked on the cuffs around the woman's wrists.

As soon as the cuffs were off, the woman pulled off her gag. "Thank you."

"Don't thank me yet," Cady said, knowing that this was far from over. "Are you okay?"

The woman didn't say anything. Cady knew the truth. These women were far from okay. She could only imagine what they'd been through.

The cuffs came off one by one. Slowly. Painfully.

But they were off. And the women were rubbing their arms, crying, hugging each other.

"Please, help us get out of here," the gaunt woman she rescued first said.

Cady glanced at her watch. "We have an hour until these guys get back. Listen to me, and listen closely. Go left out the hallway and exit the door at the end. You'll be in an alley. Go to the street corner, to the right, and into a restaurant called Sidewalk Joe's. I know the man who works there, and he'll help you. Do you understand?"

The women nodded. No, these weren't women. They were girls. Teenagers. Had Raul lured them off the streets? Had he promised them a better life only to take them captive?

Cady couldn't stomach the thought.

Just then, she heard a sound outside the door and froze.

A footfall.

Was Sloan back?

She put a hand to her lips, motioning—pleading with—the women to be quiet.

One of them held back a cry. Another wrapped her arm around her, quietly shushing her.

What Cady wouldn't do to help them. To *really* help. To give them hugs, and food, and a clean place to stay.

The bigger picture, she reminded herself.

She hated that phrase more and more every day. It seemed a crime to sacrifice anyone. There were no little people in this world. Cady was convinced that everyone mattered.

Right now, these women mattered. They mattered to her.

She pressed her ear to the door. Silence stretched on the other side.

What if Sloan was lingering in the hallway? If he caught Cady in here . . . she'd be a dead woman. She wouldn't be much help to anyone, including these women, if she died.

She counted to thirty. Then she slowly opened the door.

She scanned left. Scanned right. It was clear down the dim, dank hallway.

With her throat tight, she motioned for the ladies to exit.

"Remember what I told you," she whispered. "I'm going to go distract the guys who are here. Be quick."

"Thank you," the first blonde said, her eyes hollow. "Thank you."

"You can thank me by getting out of here alive. Now go."

The woman nodded and rushed behind the rest of the group. Each appeared skeletal as they hurried away, most likely shells of who they'd once been.

Cady could understand that. Because, at times, she also felt like a shell. Just one piece in a game that she wanted out of.

But there was no turning back now, for better or for worse.

"Anyone know what happened?" Raul barked.

Cady, Orion, Sloan, and two others were gathered around him. Sweat covered the man's forehead and his pupils were dilated—he'd obviously just taken a hit of flakka. He'd gone ballistic when he learned the women were gone, and he looked like he was about to fly off the handle again.

"I saw Sloan going down that hallway." The words nearly caught in Cady's throat. "Twice."

"Were you watching him?" Raul's beady eyes fixated on her.

Cady raised her head. "As a matter of fact, I was. Something struck me as off about him."

"Oh, no, girlie. You're not throwing me under the bus—" Sloan started, stepping toward Cady with a look of pure vengeance in his eyes.

Raul raised a hand to Sloan's chest and stopped him in his tracks. "Let the lady talk."

The pressure of the moment pushed down on Cady. If she wasn't careful, this could end badly. Very badly.

"He's seemed secretive," she said. "So I decided to keep an eye on him."

"Did you know about the women?"

"Not until I followed him. I was on my way to do the deal across town, but as I was leaving, I saw him head downstairs."

"If she's your right-hand woman, why isn't she always with you?" Sloan demanded. "Why do you trust her so much? Just because she saved your life? How do you know that wasn't a fluke?"

Raul's eyes turned as cold as black ice on an otherwise sunny day. "I trust my gut."

Sloan sneered. "And what is your gut telling you right now?"

"That you can't be trusted."

Cady held her breath, watching how things would play out. She couldn't let Sloan take the rap for this. Yet what choice did she have? Sloan was an evil man. He deserved to pay.

But this wasn't the way she liked to do things.

She needed out of the situation. Pronto.

She wasn't made to deceive people like this.

"Take him to the room where we kept the ladies," Raul said. "I need to show him a thing or two."

Raul's henchmen took Sloan's arms.

"No, man! You don't know what you're doing. I didn't do this!" Sloan's death glare kept returning to Cady.

If he survived this, he would kill her.

Her blood pressure rose so quickly she could hear air *whooshing* in her ears.

"Take care of him," Raul said. "I'll be down in a few to make sure you do a good job."

And that was the last time Cady ever saw Sloan or heard the man's name mentioned.

Chapter Twenty-Five

TODAY'S GOALS: CELEBRATE THE US OF A. PRETEND I
DIDN'T KISS TY. STAY ALIVE.

CASSIDY HAD AWAKENED with one certainty this morning. She was dangerously close to blowing her cover. With every mystery she solved, she came closer to showing her hand. Ty was already suspicious, and it wouldn't be long before he started to put things together. If she didn't handle the mystery around these ladies carefully, she was going to find herself looking for a new place to call home. She wasn't ready for that.

She'd woken early and fixed the ladies breakfast. She'd talked to them some more and tried to reassure them. None of them looked convinced. In fact, they each seemed to be growing more agitated in their own ways. Rose was becoming angrier. Kat more withdrawn. And Trina seemed to be growing more anxious by the moment.

She'd never been great at small talk, but as

Cassidy glanced out the front window and felt the sun's rays already warming the glass there, she couldn't help but remark, "It's going to be a scorcher today."

And it was the Fourth of July, which meant everyone would be outside. If she was truly an entrepreneur who loved selling ice cream, she'd bring in big bucks today selling red, white, and blue bomb pops.

Unfortunately, her mind was on other things.

"I just want to see the beach," Trina suddenly announced.

"It's not a good idea." Rose's voice sounded stern, like a general in the middle of battle. "We should stay inside."

"I'm inclined to agree with her," Cassidy said, crossing the room until she stood next to Trina. "The longer you can conceal yourself, the better."

"Just one glimpse from the deck won't hurt anything," Trina continued, fanning her face. "I'm going stir-crazy. I feel like I'm a prisoner again."

"Get over it," Rose said. "Whining never makes anything better."

Before anyone realized what she was doing, Trina rushed toward the door and threw it open.

As soon as she did, she screamed and jumped back. Had those men returned? Had they found her?

"Trina!" Rose rushed. "What is it?"

Cassidy reached for a gun that she didn't have on

her. Instead, she pushed down her alarm and peered around Trina.

Ty stood at the door.

The wrinkle in the skin between his eyes only emphasized how his gaze was full of questions and confusion.

And rightfully so.

"It's okay, guys." Cassidy's stomach sank with dread. "He's my friend. Just let me talk to him for a minute."

"Are you sure you can trust him?" Rose's voice was just above a hiss as her gaze bore a laser beam-like hole into Ty.

"You can trust him. I promise." Even though Cassidy hadn't trusted him with her own secret. The irony wasn't lost on her, yet she kept her mouth shut.

"I told you it was a bad idea to go outside." Rose turned toward Trina, shooting daggers with her eyes.

Cassidy stepped outside to meet Ty, closing the door behind her.

How was she going to explain this to him?

His gaze latched onto hers. "You have guests," he started, his voice dry.

"I do." She nodded curtly, still gathering her thoughts.

He shrugged, his head pulled to the side as if searching for words amidst his confusion. "Care to tell me where they're from?"

Cassidy licked her lips. "It's—"

"Let me guess. It's a long story."

"It is, actually."

He crossed his good arm over his slung-up one. "I'd feel better if you offered a little more information. Although I realize it's none of my business."

She glanced behind her, checking to see if the women were nearby or pressing their faces against the glass. She didn't see them. She could only imagine the heated conversation going on inside.

She pulled Ty toward the railing, away from any listening ears, just to be safe. "Look, I promised not to share details."

He squinted. "Why not?"

Cassidy let out a long breath, hating being between a rock and a hard place. "There are some bad people looking for those ladies."

"So you took them in?" His voice held an air of disbelief and wonder and . . . admiration?

Cassidy rubbed her temples, her elbows letting out a burst of pain to remind her of last night's injury. "Something like that."

"Is this connected with what happened yesterday evening?"

Cassidy nodded slowly, figuring she could admit that much. "It is."

"Cassidy . . ." He ran a hand over his face, clearly exasperated.

"Look, I know how this seems." She stepped closer and lowered her voice. "But I couldn't turn them away. They needed someone, and I was here."

He shifted his weight to his other foot, still

appearing unconvinced. "So, let me get this straight. You solved the island's first murder in thirty years. Then you helped Skye and uncovered a drug deal. Now you've found some troubled women and are helping them?"

Cassidy nodded, like it wasn't a big deal. "That's correct. The truth is . . . I get bored, and this is what I do."

He tilted his head, studying her openly and without apology. "Is that right?"

"It is."

He stepped closer and reached for her, squeezing her arm. "Cassidy Livingston . . . you're going to get yourself killed one day."

If he only knew about the million-dollar bounty on her head. "Maybe."

"I don't even know what to say."

She desperately wanted him to see her perspective. She wasn't sure why his approval was important to her. Maybe because her father had never approved? Maybe because it would be nice to have one male in her life who appreciated her?

"Look, Ty, these women are scared," she said. "If those men find them . . ."

"Let me guess—these are the same men you ran into last night, the ones who almost abducted you."

"You're correct."

"Why didn't you tell me?" A touch of hurt entered his voice.

"Because I promised them I wouldn't. I was trying

to keep my word, Ty. Believe me, I wanted to. There are things I want to tell you." She hadn't intended to say that. She held her breath as she waited for his reaction.

His gaze zoomed in on her until she was unable to look away. "Other things?"

"No. Not other things. I mean, I'm sure there are other things. But right now I'm talking about this thing." *Get a grip, Cassidy.*

"Well, maybe we can talk about those other things sometime."

She swallowed hard, desperately wishing she could, that it could be her reality. "Maybe. But one thing at a time."

Right then, her cell rang. Perfect timing, because she wanted out of this conversation before she said something she shouldn't.

"What's going on, Serena?" Cassidy paced away from Ty, her gaze going to the waves. They easily looked ten feet high. The tropical depression had turned into tropical storm. Wouldn't hit land but was stirring up surf—which meant more people would forgo the beach in favor of the parade today.

"Hey, guess what? An article just came out in the paper this morning—not the island newspaper, but the *Washington Post* newspaper—saying that Martin

Chaser is being investigated for drugs. Can you believe it?"

Martin Chaser? Maybe he *was* their guy. "No, I can't believe that."

"I just heard. I want to go ambush him and see what he says."

Cassidy cringed at the thought of it. "I don't know if that's a good idea, Serena."

"I think it's a great idea, and Ernestine agrees. It would make for riveting news, she said."

Cassidy really needed to meet Ernestine sometime. "You could be putting yourself in danger."

Ty gave her a look, and Cassidy shrugged, not in the mood to face the mirror of truth in her words.

"He eats at the Crazy Chefette every day," Serena said. "The confrontation will be in public and safe. I promise."

"Let me go with you, at least."

"You want to go with me?" Surprise laced Serena's voice.

"Well, I just don't want to see you in a bad situation. There's safety in numbers."

"Okay then. I won't turn down help. How about in an hour?"

"An hour is great. It will give us time to avoid the 5K runners. I'll meet you outside the restaurant, okay?"

"Sounds good. See you then, Cassidy."

She hung up and looked at Ty, who was patiently

waiting. "Serena wants to ambush Martin Chaser, and I told her it wasn't a good idea."

"Martin Chaser? The racecar driver?"

"He's the one."

"He's in town?" Ty really had been out of the loop while he was in the clinic.

"Going to be the Grand Marshal of the parade," Cassidy said.

He squinted and leaned against railing. "And why would Serena ambush him?"

Cassidy explained.

"You know that advice you gave Serena?"

Cassidy rubbed her chin, determined not to make this easy on him. "Which bit?"

"About putting herself in danger?"

Cassidy nodded. "Yes, I did say that."

"Maybe you should take that advice yourself."

"I'm just trying to protect Serena."

He leaned closer. "And who's going to protect you?"

"Are you volunteering?" Her voice lilted as a rush of air left her lungs.

Ty reached for her waist and tugged her closer. "I think someone needs to."

"I don't know. I can be a lot of trouble." *Stop using that voice, Cassidy. Stop it!*

"I can't argue with that." Ty brushed the hair away from her forehead.

Her heart pounded at his closeness, as she remembered their kiss last night. As she wanted another one.

Just then, the door opened behind them. Cassidy jumped back and saw Rose standing there.

"Is he harassing you?" Her dark gaze shifted to Ty.

"Who? Ty? No." Cassidy laughed at the thought of Rose attacking Ty. Then again, Rose was pretty street savvy. Maybe it wouldn't be so funny. "Well, maybe. But in a good way."

Rose eyeballed him, her upper lip twitching. "Are you sure we can trust this guy?"

Cassidy nodded, resting a hand on his chest. "Yeah, I'm sure."

Rose's demeanor softened as she turned toward him. "You better not tell anyone you saw us. If those guys find us, we're dead meat. Or even worse. They'll keep us alive and sell us like cows at an auction."

"We're not going to let that happen," Ty said, his eyes taking on a protective gleam.

Cassidy swallowed hard before speaking again. "There's one thing, though. I think we should move you to a new location."

"Why?" Distrust dripped from her voice.

"Those guys saw my face last night. If they figure out who I am, they'll find you. But I know of someone you can stay with. He'd protect you."

"How can you be sure?" Rose's eyes narrowed with challenge.

"Because I have good instincts." Except when it came to romance. Cassidy didn't need to mention that.

Rose raised her shoulder in a half shrug. "We don't have much choice but to trust you. We're at your mercy."

"Then, please, believe me. If I thought you could stay here and be safe, I'd let you. Let me make a phone call."

"Fine. I hope you're right."

———

Ty rode with Cassidy in her ice cream truck. The ladies were in the back, where no one could see them. They snacked on chocolate crunch bars to occupy themselves.

Cassidy was learning that ice cream made everything better.

And, just in case she ran into those men, Cassidy had donned a baseball cap and some oversized aviator glasses. She'd used makeup to conceal her bruises and had worn a thin, long sleeved shirt to cover the scabs on her elbows.

Hopefully those guys wouldn't recognize her. It *had* been dark outside last night. Then again, optimism had never kept anyone alive. Not in her experience, at least.

At Mac's place, she and Ty ushered the women inside. Cassidy knew they would be safe there—much safer than they'd be at Cassidy's.

"Sounds like we need to talk later," Mac said.

"I didn't mean to interrupt you as you study the

evacuation plans for the island in case of an emergency," Cassidy said. That's what he'd told her he was doing when she'd called.

"It's always best to be prepared," he said.

"I couldn't agree more," Cassidy said. "And I promise to fill you in soon. Just keep an eye on them until then, okay? They're scared . . . and in danger."

He winked at her. "I've got this."

And he did. Mac lived for stuff like this.

Knowing they were protected, Cassidy and Ty then took off for the Crazy Chefette. All around them, the town was bustling as they got ready for the activities taking place later that day. People walked down the sidewalks carrying flags. Chairs had already been set up to reserve the best seats for the parade. A gigantic sign advised visitors that the highway would be closed for three hours later today.

"So what do you think we should do when we get there? Should we confront Martin?" Cassidy asked. She already knew what she wanted to do.

She wanted to confront Martin Chaser, of course.

"Probably not the best course of action." Ty rubbed his injured shoulder again. "I think we can find out what we need to know without getting in his face. That should be the last resort."

"Okay. If you think so." She gripped the steering wheel, ignoring someone who tried to flag her down for ice cream. She didn't have time for that now.

Ty cast her a glance, as if her words surprised him. "That was easy."

She shrugged. "I'm no expert at these things, and you have fought terrorists."

"Yet strangely you seem like an expert sometimes."

His words jolted her, and she struggled to keep her expression placid. "It's like I said, I read a lot of novels. Maybe I even have good instinct—in a very civilian way."

He raised his eyebrows quickly, as if less certain than Cassidy about her theory. "I guess so. But it's been a good thing you've been around these past several weeks. You've helped bring some really bad dudes to justice."

"I knew I was here for a reason. That, and selling ice cream."

At that moment, Elsa began playing "Battle Hymn of the Republic." Cassidy hit the button to stop the music before she drew any more attention than necessary to herself and the truck. It took three tries before the music stopped.

"She really does have a mind of her own, doesn't she?" Ty said.

"You can say that again."

"I could look at her for you, if you wanted," Ty said. "Although part of her intrigue is the fact that she malfunctions for you."

"Intrigue? You mean part of what makes her annoying."

Ty cast her a grin as they pulled up to the restaurant, but it faded. "Listen, should we talk about last night?"

Cassidy's breath caught. She'd known it was coming sooner or later. She'd hoped for later. "Why don't we deal with one problem at a time?"

"Problem?" Ty asked.

Why had she said that? She nibbled on her bottom lip a moment. "Obstacle?"

"Kissing me is an obstacle?"

He had no idea. And her choice of words wasn't making any of this better. "Could we just talk later?"

"We can. But can I just make it clear that I didn't find anything about kissing you a problem or an obstacle."

Her cheeks flushed. She reached up and brushed her fingers against Ty's jaw, his cheek.

"I . . ." she started. But her words faltered.

Ty took her hand and kissed her fingers. "We'll talk later."

Relief filled her. "Let's do that. And, for now, let's go see if Serena is here."

Chapter Twenty-Six

CASSIDY AND TY slid into the booth at the Crazy Chefette beside Serena and Martin.

Maybe on another day, they could have been subtle and taken a seat behind them, but today the place was packed with Fourth of July visitors who'd rushed to the Crazy Chefette to try Lisa's red velvet pancakes with blueberries and whipped cream. Or her blue eggs, red gravy ham, and white bread. Or the blue-and-white potato gnocchi with fresh red tomato sauce.

Martin's eyes widened in surprise at their intrusion.

Cassidy got a better look at the man, noting that he was more diminutive than she would have guessed. His hair was already thinning, and his gaze lacked confidence.

Both Martin and Serena's eyes widened in

surprise as they turned from their conversation toward Ty and Cassidy.

"Fancy seeing you here," Cassidy said, keeping her voice light. "You're that racecar driver, right?"

Martin's chest puffed out. "That's correct."

"That's so cool that you're here in town," Cassidy said, making sure to sound impressed.

"Yeah, I'm a big fan," Ty said.

"Mr. Chaser was just telling me that he was asked not to be the Grand Marshal of the parade after all," Serena said. "The offer was rescinded."

"What? Why would they do that?" Cassidy's mouth gaped open.

"All because of those allegations." Martin's gaze darkened. "All someone has to do is say the word, and you're guilty before charged. I'm not involved in drugs."

"I heard you were buying an island. I thought that was so cool. I mean, who can afford an island."

Martin's expression darkened. "Correction: I *wanted* to buy an island. Do you know how expensive they are? And no, I wasn't selling drugs to try and fund it."

"Why do the police think you're not telling the truth?" Cassidy asked.

"Great question. Look, I'm broke. I've made some poor choices in my life. Some of those choices might involve a little bit of gambling—poker is one nasty habit. Believe me."

"Why'd you come here to Lantern Beach of all places?" Ty asked.

"Because it's cheap." Martin sighed. "Look, I drive an expensive car so I can impress the ladies while I'm out, but I'm staying in a dump over on Sea Oats Drive."

Cassidy's eyes widened with realization.

That was the car she'd seen. She wouldn't have pegged Martin as a Lexus guy. No, she would have guessed a sports car.

"Why a Lexus?" she asked.

"How did you know I drove a Lexus?" Martin looked at her, his gaze accusatory—yet so exaggerated that it was almost amusing. "Are you following me?"

"I just happened to be on that street and noticed the mismatched car and house. I used to be an interior designer back in the day, so I notice these things." That was another part of her cover story.

"Okay, I actually borrowed it from my dad." He scowled. "There, are you happy?"

"I don't know if I'd say happy. I mean, puppies make me happy." Cassidy nearly rolled her eyes at herself.

"My career is tanking, my finances are laughable, and my girlfriend left me. I really don't have much going for me at this point." He pushed his plate away, only half of his red velvet pancakes gone.

"I'm sorry to hear that," Ty said.

Cassidy's gaze went to Martin's arm. There was no tattoo.

Things weren't looking good for the investigation. Unless something turned around, those three women were going to be in hiding for a long time.

A table opened up across the room at the Crazy Chefette, and Ty and Cassidy grabbed it, along with two menus. Since the place seemed short-staffed, they both ordered coffee—something easy.

As they waited for it to arrive, Ty studied Cassidy, noted the determination in her eyes. The intelligence and purpose behind her words and actions. The way she sat like a soldier, watching, observing, formulating.

Something felt unsettled in Ty's gut, like Cassidy's secrets were a chasm he'd never be able to cross. Yet he couldn't deny what an important part of his life the woman had become.

She held up her phone. "Your mom seems to be doing well. She texted again."

Ty nodded. "I couldn't be happier about that. But that doesn't mean it's not going to get harder before it gets easier."

"That's true."

Ty knew what Cassidy was doing—she was trying to change the subject, to avoid the hard questions. And, as much as he would love to talk about his mom, there were other more pressing issues at the moment.

"Tell me what you know about all of this," he said.

Cassidy rubbed her lips together silently a minute before saying, "Your arm hurts. You really should rest."

He leaned closer. "You were really good back there at acting clueless, you know."

That fact hadn't gone unnoticed. And it was another part of the reason he felt unsettled right now.

Her cheeks turned red. "I may have done some acting in high school. And I know what people's misconceptions about blondes can be. I was just using that to my advantage."

What kind of act was Cassidy putting on for him? Or was she? Because there were moments when he got glimpses of Cassidy with her guard down. Those times, he felt like he saw the real person.

Then moments like these arose and threw everything Ty thought he knew into a tailspin.

"The guy behind this is called the Cobra," Cassidy finally said, almost sounding reluctant. "He apparently owns an island somewhere south of here. Most likely the Wilmington area."

"There's nothing else distinguishable about him?"

Cassidy shrugged. "He has a cobra tattoo on his arm."

He blanched. "A cobra tattoo?"

She tilted her head. "Is that familiar?"

"Renee said she saw someone in the clinic with a snake tattoo," Ty said. "Said he looked scary."

Cassidy straightened, a new light entering her

eyes. "That fits what I know. Someone told me he injured himself. Did she say anything else about him?"

"I didn't think to ask." He paused before his next suggestion. "I could call her and see if she'll talk."

Cassidy's eyes widened, almost as if he'd just suggested putting a call into the president himself. "You'd do that?"

"To save the lives of three women?" He nodded. "Of course I would. The question is, will Renee talk to me?"

"That's an excellent question."

"Let me try." He pulled out his phone and dialed her number. Just as he suspected might happen, it went to voicemail. He left a message, hung up, and then turned to Cassidy. "Maybe she'll call back."

"We can only hope. I'm not sure anyone at the clinic would give up any information about him, not with all the privacy laws."

"You're right. If Renee doesn't come through, it seems nearly impossible that we'll find this guy here," Ty said. "Especially with the crowds like we have on the Fourth of July."

"You were a SEAL. You guys rooted out terrorists from the earth's innards. Don't you have some tricks up your sleeve?"

Their coffee arrived, and he took a long sip of his. "It sounds so dramatic when you say it like that."

"But it's true, isn't it?"

Ty couldn't be sure, but there may have been a gleam of admiration in Cassidy's eyes. "The difference is that we had technology and an army of people backing us up. We don't have that here. Tell me again why we can't go to the police with this?"

Cassidy frowned and stared into her coffee a moment. "The ladies said that one of the men involved was an officer."

He didn't like the sound of that. "Would they recognize him?"

"They said they saw him from far away, but they don't trust law enforcement, and I can't blame them." She leaned closer. "You remember that night we went to the lighthouse, Ty? We saw a cop on the shoreline doing something that seemed pretty unsavory."

"Yes, we did." He hadn't stopped thinking about the encounter since. "There's a chance that one of the cops here is involved with something. We just don't know who. Quinton? Bozeman? Leggott?"

"Exactly. But we might want to keep that in mind as we move forward." She drew in a long breath. "Speaking of which . . . where *do* we go from here?"

He leaned back and tried to think everything through. "Do you know anything else about the man, other than he's evil, rich, and ruthless, with a cobra tattoo?"

"Only that he liked to eat . . ." Lisa appeared at the table, as if right on cue. Cassidy turned toward her. "Lisa, has anyone requested liver and onions here lately?"

She shrugged, as if the question wasn't unusual.

"As a matter of fact, they have. It's funny that you ask."

"Do you remember who?"

Lisa thought about it a moment. "You know, I really don't. I didn't recognize him. Nor did I think it was a big deal, truth be told."

Cassidy and Ty exchanged a look.

Lisa shifted her weight from one hip to the other. "Why? What's going on?"

Cassidy shook her head. The problem with asking questions was that it caused other people to also ask questions. "Just wondering. It's a long story, but I'll explain when I can."

"Do you two want to try some?"

"No, thank you," Ty and Cassidy said at the same time.

"If you change your mind, let me know. I make this recipe with liver and Brussel sprouts that's out of this world."

"Why are you shorthanded today?" Cassidy asked.

"My new waitress, Melissa, requested the day off." Lisa frowned. "I usually don't give holidays off, but what can I say? I'm a softie. She met this guy, and he's coming into town today. She was over-the-moon excited about it."

"A guy?" Cassidy asked.

Lisa nodded. "She met him online, apparently. I guess that's the new way to do things."

"Do you know where they were meeting, Lisa?" Urgency and concern hitched Cassidy's voice.

Lisa shrugged. "Not really. I think it was on the boardwalk somewhere. Why? What's wrong?"

Cassidy stood. "It's a long story. But you should call her. Tell her not to go anywhere alone with this guy."

"Okay, you're making me nervous."

"Let's just say she fits the profile of someone who . . . well, who could disappear forever. Her online date most likely knows that too."

Chapter Twenty-Seven

"MAYBE WE SHOULD SPLIT UP," Cassidy said as she and Ty climbed back into Elsa.

"I'm not sure that's a good idea." Ty twisted his head, his neck and shoulders tight with disagreement —and possibly discomfort. "Besides, we need to find somewhere to park. The highway is closed for the parade."

"Niles said I could sell ice cream. I should be able to get past those barricades."

"*Are* you going to sell ice cream?"

"Of course not. I've got to find Melissa."

"Let's stay together for as long as we can, okay?" Ty said. "I'd feel a lot better if we worked as a team, especially since these guys are looking for you. If they find you again . . ."

Cassidy shivered at the thought of it. She didn't want them to find her either, not after last time. "Okay, that's fine. Let's go."

Just as she'd hoped, a volunteer let her through the barricade before the parade started. She found a place on a public lot and parked. As she and Ty climbed out, several people asked about buying ice cream. Cassidy insisted to them she'd be back later.

Maybe.

For now, she and Ty paused on the sidewalk and glanced around.

Everyone had begun lining up for the parade at the school's athletic fields. Maybe that would be the best place to start.

She'd only taken two steps when she ran into a familiar figure.

"Hey, there, Quinton," she said, trying not to look uneasy around him.

"Hey, Katniss."

"Cassidy," she corrected.

"That's right. Cassidy." He smiled, clueless as to how annoyed Cassidy felt every time he got her name wrong.

"Hey, I'm glad I ran into you. I was wondering if the Coast Guard ever took that raft away? I heard Niles wanted to put it in the parade, and my friend Ty over here wanted to see it."

Quinton nodded a stiff hello to Ty before shaking his head. "Actually, they didn't. Officer Savage found some kind of evidence onboard but left the raft itself. Said we could dispose of it as we saw fit."

Ty stepped closer, that intimidating Navy SEAL look on his face. "What kind of evidence?"

Quinton shrugged. "Looked like a piece of jewelry or a compass or something. I didn't ask any questions."

Cassidy's heart quickened. Was it the locket Trina had left with the coordinates to the island? She needed to know what he'd found. The coast-guardsman may have all the answers Cassidy was looking for and not even realize it.

"The Coast Guard has a unit in the parade," Quinton continued. "If you're really curious, you could find them and ask. Doubt they'll tell you anything, though."

"Thanks a bunch." She smiled before walking away with Ty and lowering her voice. "We need to find him, Ty."

"I thought we needed to find Melissa."

"Both."

He sighed. "This is where you want to split up, isn't it?"

She nodded. "I'm sorry. But I'll be safe. I promise."

"I don't like this." A storm raged inside his eyes.

"Remember, we have a conversation to have later."

"You mean, the one that's a problem?"

She smiled. "That's the one. I intend on staying alive so we can have it."

His worried gaze latched onto hers. "I'm going to hold you to that, Cassidy."

"Please do. Now, let's go. I'll stay in touch."

Ty paused on the boardwalk, which, at the moment, was an overstimulating playground of sensory items. Crowds laughed and cheered. The heat made the air feel like a sauna. The smell of hot dogs and popcorn wafted, making his stomach rumble.

His shoulder ached, but he ignored the pain as he glanced around, looking for someone who matched the description that Cassidy had given him. There were a lot of people to sort through, and Ty couldn't stop worrying about Cassidy. He didn't like the fact that they'd split up, especially not with those men who'd hurt her last night still on the loose. But he could tell he wasn't going to be able to talk her out of it.

His phone rang in his pocket. He pulled it out and glanced at the screen. It was Renee. Was she actually calling him back?

Her voice sounded cold on the other line. "You called?"

"Renee, I need your help." He felt bad about the way things had ended but trying to tell her nicely hadn't worked.

"I offered you my help and you rejected it." Derision and hurt dripped from her voice.

"Listen, this is important. Life or death. Okay?"

She sighed. "What is it?"

"You told me you saw someone in the clinic with a cobra tattoo, correct?"

"Yeah. You didn't seem all that interested at the time." Derision and hurt morphed into accusation. A scorned woman was not a fun woman to work with.

Ty didn't have time to play these games. "What did he look like, Renee? We think he's a bad man who's about to strike again—to strike an innocent girl who thinks she's looking for a love connection."

"That's horrible. No one should have her heart broken like that."

It had been another jab directed at him. Ty remained silent, waiting for her to do the right thing. Certainly she had enough of a moral compass to know how serious this was.

Finally, she sighed again. "I don't remember exactly what he looked like. He had huge arms and muscles. Cold eyes. But when he smiled, everything about him warmed up. He was an odd mix of attributes, I guess. Or maybe he could just turn the charm —or lack thereof—on and off. I didn't see his hair. He wore a hat."

"Good to know."

"I overheard some nurses saying he had a nasty cut and that it was at least a day old. Oh, and one other thing I do remember," Renee continued, obviously liking the fact that she had all the power in the conversation.

"What is it?"

"He was carrying a bag with him, but I could see something peeking out of it. It looked like a uniform of some sort."

Ty paused as her words sank in. "What kind of uniform, Renee? Mechanic? Doctor? What?"

"No, like law enforcement, if I had to guess."

Ty thanked Renee and hung up. He didn't like the sound of this. Not at all.

Cassidy's phone rang, and she saw it was Lisa. She shoved the phone to her ear as she walked.

"What's going on?" Cassidy skirted past the crowds of innocent bystanders who had no idea of the evil going on here in Lantern Beach. She almost envied their naivety for a minute. She'd seen too much to ever feel that relaxed.

"I called Melissa," Lisa said. "But she's not answering. I'm getting nervous."

She scanned the crowds, looking for anything suspicious. But mostly what she saw was expected—the crowds carrying chairs to the parade route. Little kids perched on their father's shoulders. People sporting American flags and smiles.

"Ty and I are out here looking for her," Cassidy told Lisa.

"What's wrong, Cassidy? What's going on?"

She cut through a parking lot to cut some distance off the trek. "We think there's a predator here on the island who targets women he meets through online dating."

Lisa gasped. "That's terrible. You think Melissa is

one of those women?"

"Possibly. That's why we're trying to find her. If she tries to leave with him . . ."

"I'll go and help you. I should have never given her the day off."

"You couldn't have known," Cassidy said, dodging through more crowds. She finally reached the staging area for the parade. "You should stay at the Crazy Chefette, just in case she returns."

"But . . ."

The last thing Cassidy needed was for Lisa to get hurt. "You won't be able to get past the barricades now anyway. Listen, I need to go. Keep me updated, and I'll do the same."

She shoved her phone back into her pocket and paused as something in the distance caught her eye. Two teens knelt beside a police cruiser . . . with spray paint in hand.

"Hey!" she called.

The teens saw her, and their eyes widened. They dropped the spray paint and ran.

Ordinarily, Cassidy might chase them. But today she had bigger fish to fry. Instead, she grabbed the paint cans and slipped them into her purse. No need to add litter to the crimes around here. Besides, maybe those kids' prints were on these cans.

As she reached the school's athletic fields, she paused and glanced around. There was a high school marching band, a dance group, a club driving miniature cars, people on horses, and too many others to even mention.

So where was the Coast Guard?

She spotted a group in white uniforms in the distance. That had to be them.

She rushed through the crowds until she reached them. She searched the faces but didn't spot Savage. What if he wasn't marching? She had to get in touch with him somehow.

Finally, she tapped one of the men on the shoulder. "Excuse me."

The man turned and smiled. "Yes?"

She tapped into all her blondeness and smiled sweetly. "Excuse me. I'm looking for Savage. Is he here?"

A strange expression crossed his face. He nodded toward a man three people over. "He's right there."

Cassidy's gaze swerved toward the man.

But this Savage wasn't the same Savage she'd talked to at the police station.

Her heart pounded in her ears.

No, that man hadn't been Coast Guard at all, had he?

Chapter Twenty-Eight

AS CASSIDY STARTED BACK toward the boardwalk, her cell rang again. This time it was Ty.

"I see Melissa," he said. "There's a man approaching."

She remembered the man who'd pretended to be a Coastie. "Is he a big guy with blond hair?"

"No, he's tall with dark hair. Is he the guy you're looking for?"

"I'm nearly certain he works for the Cobra," Cassidy said. He could even be one of the men who'd tried to abduct her.

"I'll go keep him away from her."

"No, wait," Cassidy said, scenarios playing out in her mind. That wasn't the direction they needed to go. Not yet, at least. "You don't want to scare him away. We need him to be arrested and off the streets."

"How do you propose we do that?"

She nibbled on her bottom lip, thankful that Ty

was letting her take the lead. Not all men—especially alpha males—would be okay with that. "Where are you, exactly?"

"Near The Docks restaurant."

"Keep an eye on them. In fact, don't let them out of your sight. I'm going to put in a tip to the police."

"You think that will be enough to stop this?" An edge of skepticism entered his voice.

"I'm hoping it will be. Otherwise, start thinking about a backup plan."

"I'll trust you on this one," he said. "Keep me updated."

"Will do. I'm headed toward you now."

As soon as she hung up, she dialed the police. Dispatch answered. "There's a man who was imitating a coastguardsman. He's now harassing a girl with long, dark hair outside The Docks restaurant. They need an officer there right away."

Before dispatch could ask any more questions, Cassidy hung up. And then she slid back into the crowds, making her way toward Ty.

Five minutes later, she found him concealed behind the corner of a gift shop. The town's local singer/songwriter, Carter Denver, played the guitar and sang "Only in America" across the path. If she wasn't on a mission, she might take a moment to enjoy the music and maybe to even tell Ty how much she appreciated the sacrifices he'd made for the country. But this wasn't the time.

"Are they still there?" she asked, following Ty's gaze.

Ty nodded in the distance. "They've just been talking. They look . . . happy."

"That's all part of the show." When she thought of how these men took advantage of the women's loneliness, another surge of anger rushed through her.

Cassidy zeroed in on the man. She instantly recognized him as the man who'd tried to abduct her, just as she'd suspected. She glanced around and spotted another man in the distance. He stood casually on the boardwalk, sipping a smoothie and wearing sunglasses.

"He's one of them also," Cassidy said, nodding across the way.

"Very observant." Ty glanced around. "Any more?"

"Not that I see right now. The police should be showing up any time now. I just hope they don't blow it." If it was Bozeman and Quinton, there was a good chance that would happen.

"Well, I heard a couple of people walking past saying there was a brawl between two of the ballet teachers. The police could be occupied with that now."

Just then, Melissa and the man stood from the bench. She slipped her arm through his, and they began to stroll down the boardwalk.

No, no, no . . .

This couldn't happen.

"We've got to follow them." Ty bristled beside her.

"Yes, we do." As soon as she said the words, the sound of the marching band filled the air, drowning out the noise of the crowds. The parade was starting.

Things had just gotten ten times more complicated.

Cassidy and Ty wove their way into the crowd, staying a safe distance behind Melissa and the man. As they walked farther down the boardwalk, the crowds thickened, rushing toward the parade route. Cassidy stood on her tiptoes, trying to keep Melissa in sight.

They were going toward the parking lot, she realized.

There weren't but so many places they could go if they got into a car. The streets were closed.

Then again, the police were occupied so this just might be the perfect time for someone to make a move. A criminal move.

"Cassidy, they're getting in a car," Ty said.

"Come on." She grabbed her keys.

"What are you doing?"

"I'm parked right over here also. We've got to follow them."

"I don't know where they think they're going to go." Ty shook his head, still looking every bit as masculine as ever, even with his arm in a sling.

"Wherever it is, we'll be right behind them."

Ty didn't argue. "Let's go then."

Ty's mind raced as he climbed into Elsa. He wished he could drive, but he was in no state to do that with his arm. Besides, Cassidy seemed to know what she was doing.

Which left him unsettled again.

He knew she had secrets. He'd found that stash of guns in her place. He'd seen her handle herself with training beyond what the average person should have. She could claim all she wanted she'd taken self-defense courses, but Ty knew there was more to the story.

Was she running from an abusive ex? It was a possibility. It would explain how jumpy she was. How she always watched everything around her. How she'd learned to defend herself.

Or what if she was a witness to a crime? That was another possibility. Or maybe she'd been accused of a crime. What if she'd come to Lantern Beach to hide? Either from law enforcement or criminals?

He wasn't sure. He only knew when he'd done an Internet search for Cassidy Livingston, none of them were for his Cassidy. And, in this day and age, that was suspicious in itself.

Ty glanced at her, noting the determination on her face. Cassidy had tried to hide it more when they'd first met. But now there was no denying it.

The woman had a penchant for justice—a fire deep inside her—that reminded him of some of the best soldiers he'd ever met. And he'd met some of the best.

When would she trust Ty enough to open up? Or would she?

"They're heading toward the lighthouse," Cassidy muttered. "There's a third man in the car. The driver. He could be the Cobra."

She was right. This road only led one place—the lighthouse and a state park beyond it. This street was otherwise deserted right now, surrounded by only trees and narrow ditches.

"And what do you plan on doing when they finally stop? I have to say that confronting him doesn't sound like the best idea." He was trying to let Cassidy take the lead here. It was her rodeo, after all. But he'd feel better if he knew the game plan.

"Confronting him is a terrible idea," Cassidy agreed. She tossed her phone toward him. "Can you call the police? Tell them that a man in a black sedan headed toward the lighthouse stole some jewelry?"

"Jewelry?"

"It's actually a locket, but jewelry sounds more extensive. I'll explain later."

He didn't bother arguing. Ty knew that Cassidy had some sort of reasoning for this. There would be time to ask about it later.

He hoped. But he desperately wanted to figure her out and put an end to his questions.

As soon as he made the call, Cassidy sped up until she was right behind the sedan.

"What are you doing?" he asked. Had she lost her mind?

"Is your seatbelt on?"

He glanced down to confirm. "Yes. Why?"

"Hold on." With steely determination, she gripped the wheel and stared ahead.

And before Ty could say anything else, Cassidy rammed Elsa into the sedan.

Chapter Twenty-Nine

THE SEDAN in front of them wobbled before jerking, pulling off to the side of the road, and coming to a stop.

Cassidy smiled. If she had to guess, the car had shut down on impact. That's what she'd been hoping for. The model was just old enough that the fuel pump should have triggered the entire vehicle to stop.

"Cassidy . . ." Ty muttered, the concern on his face causing her pulse to race. "Are you okay?"

She nodded, trying to keep her thoughts together. Having Ty here made everything so much more complicated. Yet, at the same time, so much better.

"I'm fine," she started. "Look . . . I know what I'm about to do will seem odd. I'm just trying to save a woman's life. So . . ."

His jaw tightened. "I understand. But I'm not letting you do this alone."

Cassidy released her breath. She only hoped she

didn't get him killed. And the questions he was going to ask after this . . . she wasn't sure how she would answer. But she'd cross that bridge later.

Channeling her inner ditzy blonde again, she sprang from the truck, certain to keep the cross-body purse on. She'd need it later. She rushed toward the sedan just as the driver stepped out.

"I'm so sorry," she started. "My truck takes on a mind of her own sometimes, and the brakes weren't working. It was the craziest thing. I just couldn't stop, and the accelerator jammed. So much for selling ice cream to the crowds down at the lighthouse. Is everyone okay?"

She kept her sunglasses on and her baseball cap pulled down low, just in case anyone might recognize her—including Melissa.

The man who stared back at her was definitely Savage. Or, the man who'd called himself Savage at the police station. The man also known as the Cobra.

She glanced at his arm, hoping to see a tattoo, but his shirt covered it.

However, a bandage did protrude from one of his sleeves. Was that from the cut he'd gotten while trying to abduct a woman in Myrtle Beach?

"What were you thinking?" the man demanded, hulking over her as anger shot through his words.

"Hey, hold up." Ty stepped closer. "It was an accident. The truck has been malfunctioning."

"Well, this is highly inconvenient."

"I know, and I'm so sorry," Cassidy continued.

"What can I do? How about some ice cream? My treat."

The Cobra's eyes narrowed. "No, thank you."

"How about your friends in the back? Would they like some?" She glanced in the back and saw Melissa. She couldn't get a read on the woman, though. Was she frightened? Or was she clueless about what was really happening?

The Cobra scowled again. "We're fine. I just need to get the car started. I have an appointment."

At just that moment, the police pulled up. Bozeman, just as Cassidy had hoped.

She closed her eyes a moment, hoping her plan worked. There were so many things that could go wrong.

Bozeman strode out, tucking his shirt into his pants and looking rather annoyed. "What's going on here?"

"It's all my fault, chief," Cassidy started, making sure to blather. "My brakes went out, and I ran right into this nice man and his friends. Now I've made them late, and mosquitoes are probably eating them alive."

Cassidy slapped an imaginary bug from her neck.

The chief's gaze went to Savage. "Is that correct?"

"Yes, but I'd really just like to get out of here." Savage's voice was even, but rage still simmered in his gaze. A little fender bender was stopping his grand plan—and that was exactly what Cassidy had hoped for.

A state police officer also pulled up behind them. They'd called in reinforcements for the festivities today, apparently. That was good because they needed all the help they could get right now, especially if things played out the way Cassidy hoped.

"License and registration," Bozeman said. "Why don't your friends get out of the vehicle also? I'm sure they're going to get warm in this heat."

"They're fine. This won't take long."

Cassidy glanced in the back. "No, actually the girl back there looks like she might pass out. It's probably 95 degrees out here now and with no AC . . ."

Savage scowled. "It's really not necessary."

Ty opened the door. "Of course it is. Besides, your car won't even start right now. I can take a look if you'd like."

A man climbed out, pulling Melissa beside him. Cassidy scanned them all, but she didn't see any weapons. Guns could still be concealed by the men's clothing, however.

Cassidy looked at the girl, hoping she didn't show any recognition. She didn't.

But she did look pale. She was getting the idea that these men weren't who they claimed. They'd probably told her a boatload of lies, said they were taking her to a private yacht. And she'd wanted to believe them, even though deep inside, she knew something didn't sound right.

Cassidy had heard similar stories too many times.

As they climbed out, Cassidy enacted step two of her plan.

Carefully, she leaned down. As she did, she slipped a hand into her purse, stood, and raised a spray paint can.

"Oh, look what you dropped. Some red spray paint." She giggled. "It matches the paint on your car, chief."

The chief's face went from all business to totally ticked off. "You're the ones who've been tagging my car? Calling me Bozo?"

The Cobra's eyes widened. "I have no idea where that came from."

Cassidy shrugged. "Like I said, it fell out the back when they opened the door. That's all I know."

"I'm going to have to take you in for questioning," the chief said, grabbing the Cobra's arm.

"I'm telling you, I have no idea what this is about. It's a mistake."

Cassidy tugged Melissa away from the men. "You look like you could use some ice cream."

"No, I'm . . ." she started.

"I insist." She pulled her toward the back of the truck. Ty followed.

Once they were out of sight, Cassidy lowered her voice. "If you leave with those men, no one will ever see you again. Understand?"

"You're the woman from the clinic," she muttered.

"It's a long story," Cassidy said. "But stay here."

Just as the final word left her mouth, the air around them changed.

Cassidy jerked her head toward the scene and saw that the state police had drawn their guns.

"Stay down!" Ty said, covering them with his body.

Cassidy remained behind the truck. Right now, they needed to keep Melissa safe.

Gunfire sliced through the air. Melissa let out a scream. The air lit with shots and the smoky scent of ammunition.

One of the state police officers within Cassidy's sight grabbed his arm. He'd been hit.

More shouts. More movement. More gunfire.

Ty continued to shield them from what was happening.

But Cassidy could hardly breathe. What was happening out there? She itched to be a part of it.

Finally, silence cut through the air.

An ambulance pulled up, followed by more state police.

"What's going on?" Cassidy whispered.

Ty peered out. "The man driving the car was shot, as was one other man. The third surrendered."

"Bozeman?" she asked.

"He appears to be okay."

Cassidy released her breath. Maybe everything would be okay. She could hope.

And now she needed to review her cover story because there were sure to be a lot of questions.

"So these guys were going to sell me into a human trafficking ring?" Melissa said.

They still stood behind Elsa, in an area that was shaded. Most of the other law enforcement officers were gathered by the sedan—in the area where the men had been shot. There were two ambulances behind them, however. Ty was busy filling in the gaps of conversation about what had happened with Bozeman.

Cassidy nodded in response to Melissa's question. "I'm sorry. I know you thought you'd met your perfect match. That's what they want you to think."

She frowned. "I just wanted someone to turn my life around, to get me out of this pit that's been trapping me."

"You can turn your life around. It's going to be hard. It's going to be a lot of work. But it's entirely possible."

Melissa studied her face. "Why are you so certain?"

"Because my whole life people have only liked me for what I could do for them," Cassidy whispered. "No one's ever liked me for me, and that's one of the loneliest feelings in the world. I had to walk through fire, but things are finally turning around. Besides, Lisa and I will be there for you, if you need someone."

Melissa nodded. "Thank you. I was really close to

living out a nightmare. If your ice cream truck hadn't had the brakes go out when they did . . ."

"It's a good thing Elsa has a mind of her own."

Melissa gave her a hug. "Thanks again."

She paced toward the officers, who wanted to talk to her again. While Melissa did that, Cassidy turned toward the medical personnel behind her. Most of them were busy fussing over the state police officer who'd been shot.

The Cobra was strapped to a gurney, waiting to be placed in the ambulance. No one was paying much attention to him at the moment—which meant this was Cassidy's perfect opportunity to have a chat.

"I know who you are," she whispered. "And you're not going to get away with what you've done."

He scowled. "Who are you?"

"No one important. But I know about your island. I know you kept women there. That you came here looking for your 'inventory' that got away. You're despicable."

He grunted. "You can't prove anything."

"I know you've got a cobra tattoo. And I know how you got that injury on your arm, as well. Myrtle Beach ring any bells?"

He scowled again and then spit, the liquid hitting her cheek.

Cassidy grimaced and wiped away the spittle. "The world is a better place without you as a part of it."

"You're clever. But you're not going to get away with this. I have more men, you know."

"And none of them can obviously think for themselves. If they could, they wouldn't have followed you so blindly. And I'm sure once they're pressured, they'll cave and save themselves by selling you out."

He struggled against his restraints, snarling. "If I could get my hands on you."

Ty joined her, placing a hand on Cassidy's arm. "Come on. Let's go. The police have everything they need, and they're calling the FBI in."

She gave Savage one last look before allowing Ty to pull her away. She needed to get out of here before the feds showed up. The last thing she needed was for them to nose around in her life or put her name into any type of file.

Cassidy and Ty had to go to the police station to give an official statement. Thankfully, Elsa still worked. The bumper was dented, but the girl was so old that she was made like a tank.

As they left the station and climbed back into the truck, Cassidy sensed the questions Ty must have for her. Before he could ask any of them, she blurted, "I need to go talk to the ladies at Mac's place. Are you okay with that?"

"Of course," Ty said.

But his gaze looked heavy and deep, like the questions floating there were burdens.

Cassidy understood that all too well. She wished more than anything she could pour out the truth to him. But she couldn't. Not now. Maybe not ever.

With the parade over and the streets open again, it took only five minutes to reach his place.

Mac answered the door, his eyes also full of questions. He'd obviously been listening to the police scanner. "I was itching to get out there. But I stayed here, just like I promised."

"I knew you would. Thank you," Cassidy said. "I'll explain more to you later, but could I have a moment with the ladies first?"

"Of course." He disappeared onto the deck with Ty and left Cassidy with the three women.

"What happened?" Rose demanded, crossing her arms with that same hardened look on her face.

"They caught the Cobra," Cassidy stated.

Rose's gaze softened ever-so-slightly. "Are you sure?"

Cassidy nodded and held up her phone. She'd snapped a picture of him on the gurney. "Is this him?"

Rose's eyes widened. "I'm nearly certain that's him. I mean, I didn't get a good look at him, but . . . I just know it. How . . . What . . ."

"He was posing as a coastguardsman."

"One of his friends is a cop, though," Rose said.

"How do you know?"

"I saw it out the window. Someone came to the island wearing a uniform. It wasn't the Cobra."

A looming feeling of dread swirled in Cassidy's stomach. "Now that the Cobra will be behind bars, his whole network will fall apart. More information will come out as the FBI questions him. If there is a cop working for him, his day is coming. Just give it time."

Rose rubbed her arms. "I hope so."

"Let's just say the Cobra will most likely be going away for the rest of his life. You don't have anything to be afraid of." She looked forward to the day when someone might say those same words to her. Sometimes it didn't seem like a possibility.

"I don't know how we can ever thank you," Trina said.

"There is one way," Cassidy started, her throat suddenly dry. "When you talk to the FBI—because you're going to have to talk to them—don't mention me."

"What do you mean?" Skepticism etched Rose's gaze again.

"Could you just tell them you found that abandoned house and stayed there?"

"Why wouldn't we mention you?" Rose continued.

"It's just less complicated if you leave me out."

"You did something bad, didn't you?" Rose said. "I could see it in your eyes from the moment we met."

Cassidy remembered when she'd killed Raul. She

remembered when she'd sent Sloan away, and how no one had heard from him since. How two women had been killed because they'd looked like Cassidy.

Yeah, she had done some bad things. She had regrets she'd have to live with for the rest of her life.

"I have. And I don't want the FBI poking around. Please."

Rose stared at her a minute before finally nodding. "Okay. You saved our lives. We can help you out too."

"Thank you. Now, if it's okay, I'll have Mac take you down to the station."

"He's a funny man," Kat said. "He taught us how to properly clean a gun and some basic self-defense moves."

Cassidy smiled. "That's Mac for you."

Before Cassidy realized what was happening, Rose threw her arms around her. "Thank you. We'd be dead if it wasn't for you."

"I'm glad I could help." Emotions clogged Cassidy's throat.

Kat and Trina also threw their arms around her.

Now that this was over, it was time to talk to Ty. He'd seen a side of Cassidy today that she'd tried to conceal. But he was no dummy. He had to be piecing things together.

The thought left her gut twisted into a knot because she wasn't sure what this meant for her future.

Chapter Thirty

CASSIDY HAD PROMISED to go home, get cleaned up, and then meet Ty so they could talk. It was already eight o'clock, and the sun was setting rapidly on this memorable Fourth of July.

When she stepped outside, she spotted Ty on his deck, sitting on the porch swing and waiting for her. His eyes met hers, and he waved.

With a touch of hesitation, she headed over. The night had cooled off, and the crickets were already humming. She took her time as she headed across the sand and up to his deck. She dreaded this conversation. Dreaded the questions she knew would come.

Kujo greeted her with a moist lick on the face. She rubbed his head in return and promised to play fetch later.

A book sat in Ty's lap, and his face lit with a soft grin when he saw her. On the small speakers he'd set up in the corner, patriotic music played. Mannheim Steamroller, if she had to guess.

"Hey there," he murmured.

"Hey." She sat beside him and peered over his shoulder. "You're reading."

He turned the book over so she could see the cover.

"A memoir?" she questioned. "About a man and his dog?"

"What did you expect?"

"I'm not really sure. Maybe I didn't expect you to read." She elbowed him playfully.

He clutched his heart. "Ouch."

"No offense." She smiled, letting him know she was teasing.

"No offense taken. I used to read Tom Clancy and Lee Child. After serving overseas, I couldn't read those books anymore. So I started on memoirs. They're not too bad."

"That's good to know."

"Any updates?" He turned toward her, his eyes all serious now.

"The women are being helped by the FBI," Cassidy said, a touch of apprehension in her voice. "The police found the locket with the coordinates in the car, and I heard they're sending a team to the island to make sure there are no other women there. The Cobra is behind bars."

"You did that, you know."

She shrugged. "Not really. All I did was try to help

those who needed help. It wasn't a big deal."

"I'd say it was."

Cassidy had done what needed to be done, but she wasn't sure what the outcome would be. Only time would tell.

"Smooth move with the spray paint," Ty said.

"I had to think quickly."

"You're pretty good at that."

Ty gazed at her a minute before leaning forward and planting a soft kiss on her lips. "You're beautiful, Cassidy Livingston."

She looked away and pushed a hair behind her ear. "Thank you."

"Are you blushing?" A teasing tone lilted his voice.

"Me? I don't blush." At least, she hadn't until recently.

"That's what I would have thought, but I do believe your cheeks are turning red."

"Don't flatter yourself."

He leaned close again. Close enough to touch her jaw tenderly. Close enough that his scent consumed her. "I think it's adorable."

Cassidy's heart pounded. The truth was that she felt giddy. *Giddy.* She'd never in her life felt giddy before and hardly knew what to do with it.

Accept where you are and make the most of every day. That is the definition of being happy.

"Is this where we talk about our problem?" she asked, clearing her throat before she got caught up in the moment.

Ty pulled back, his grin disappearing. "I think so."

"I feel like I should apologize for kissing you and confusing you . . . but I just can't," Cassidy admitted, startled by her own honesty. She decided to start by talking about their kiss. It seemed the easiest of the two options.

"I'm glad you're not apologizing for it."

She sucked in a shaky breath. "But the truth is . . . I don't know what's in store for my future and . . . I know you probably have a lot of questions about my past."

"Questions that you're not ready to answer," Ty said.

She swallowed hard, swinging her leg as the swing rocked back and forth. "I'm sorry, Ty. I know it doesn't help if I tell you it's complicated. But . . ."

He waited.

"Honestly, there's so much I want to say. But I can't. Not yet."

"You will when you're ready," he said.

Relief and surprise filled her at his patience. What had she ever done to meet someone as kind and honorable as Ty Chambers? She had no idea. But she felt grateful.

"Thank you," she whispered.

"Listen." He nudged her chin up. "I may not know the details about your past or what brought you here or what it is that keeps you constantly looking over your shoulder. But I do know who you are apart from those specifics. I know you have a heart of gold.

I know you make me feel things I've never felt before. That you're strong and capable and the most intriguing person I've ever met."

Tears filled her eyes. She tried to quickly brush them away, but it was too late. Ty had seen them.

He gently caressed away the moisture on her cheeks. "I didn't mean to make you tear up."

Her throat ached from all the emotions running through her. "This may not make a lot of sense, but my whole life, people have only ever liked me for the specifics of my life. You're one of the first people to ever really liked me just for me."

She'd never spoken truer words. Other than Lucy, people had always used their relationship with Cassidy to get ahead. Even Ricky Ernest had only dated her because he wanted an internship with her father's company.

Thankfully, the man—now a PI—hadn't shown up here. Yet. She'd keep her eyes open, though.

But she'd think about that another time.

Ty cupped her face. "Well, I think that's a shame because you're a beautiful person, Cassidy Livingston."

More moisture filled her eyes. "Thank you."

He lowered his head toward hers again. "That said, how about if we take it day by day?"

"Explain your definition of day by day." Her heart pounded in her ears as she waited for his response.

"I mean, let's do what you're supposed to do when dating. Let's see what's there. Then we can determine the future after that. After all, all we're guaranteed is today. You and I both know that, don't we?"

His words sounded too good to be true. Would that work? Could Cassidy actually be okay with taking things day by day, knowing that it would end with . . . with what? How would it end?

What if she did go back to Seattle and testify? What if she put away members of DH-7 for life? Was it a possibility she might be able to come back here and actually be with Ty?

She'd never thought so. Until now.

Maybe if they were meant to be together, it would work out.

"Did I leave you speechless?" Ty whispered.

"Yeah, you kind of did."

He shrugged. "I didn't know that defining dating might do that to you."

She slapped his arm—the uninjured one.

"You're always such a smart mouth." The teasing left her lips, though. "You'd really be okay with that plan? For taking it slow? Day by day? No promises about the future?"

"We're not promised the future, Cassidy. We're only promised right now."

"Okay then. Let's try the right-this-moment."

Ty grinned, and she tucked herself into him. As she did, the fireworks began exploding down the shore, bright displays of red, white, and blue.

And, for the moment, everything was perfect—perfect beyond her wildest dreams.

Coming in April:

DANGEROUS WATERS

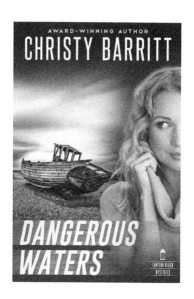

Also by Christy Barritt:

Other Books in the Lantern Beach Mystery Series:

Hidden Currents

You can take the detective out of the investigation, but you can't take the investigator out of the detective. A notorious gang puts a bounty on Detective Cady Matthews's head after she takes down their leader, leaving her no choice but to hide until she can testify at trial. But her temporary home across the country on a remote North Carolina island isn't as peaceful as she initially thinks. Living under the new identity of Cassidy Livingston, she struggles to keep her investigative skills tucked away, especially after a body washes ashore. When local police bungle the murder investigation, she can't resist stepping in. But Cassidy is supposed to be keeping a low profile. One wrong move could lead to both her discovery and her demise. Can she bring justice to the island . . . or will the hidden currents surrounding her pull her under for good?

Flood Watch

The tide is high, and so is the danger on Lantern Beach. Still in hiding after infiltrating a dangerous gang, Cassidy Livingston just has to make it a few more months before she can testify at trial and resume her old life. But trouble keeps finding her, and Cassidy is pulled into a local investigation after a man mysteriously disappears from the island she now calls home. A recurring nightmare from her time undercover only muddies things, as does a visit from the parents of her handsome ex-Navy SEAL neighbor. When a friend's life is threatened, Cassidy must make choices that put her on the verge of blowing her cover. With a flood watch on her emotions and her life in a tangle, will Cassidy find the truth? Or will her past finally drown her?

Storm Surge

A storm is brewing hundreds of miles away, but its effects are devastating even from afar. Laid-back, loose, and light: that's Cassidy Livingston's new motto. But when a makeshift boat with a bloody cloth inside washes ashore near her oceanfront home, her detective instincts shift into gear . . . again. Seeking clues isn't the only thing on her mind—romance is heating up with next-door neighbor and former Navy SEAL Ty Chambers as well. Her heart wants the love and stability she's longed for her entire life. But her hidden identity only leads to a tidal wave of turbulence. As more answers emerge about the boat, the danger around her rises, creating a treacherous swell that threatens to reveal her past. Can Cassidy mind her own business, or will the storm surge of violence and corruption that has washed ashore on Lantern Beach leave her life in wreckage?

You might also enjoy ...

On her way to completing a degree in forensic science, Gabby St. Claire drops out of school and starts her own crime-scene cleaning business. When a routine cleaning job uncovers a murder weapon the police overlooked, she realizes that the wrong person is in jail. She also realizes that crime scene cleaning might be the perfect career for utilizing her investigative skills.

You might also enjoy …

Holly Anna Paladin Mysteries:

When Holly Anna Paladin is given a year to live, she embraces her final days doing what she loves most—random acts of kindness. But when one of her extreme good deeds goes horribly wrong, implicating Holly in a string of murders, Holly is suddenly in a different kind of fight for her life. She knows one thing for sure: she only has a short amount of time to make a difference. And if helping the people she cares about puts her in danger, it's a risk worth taking.

#1 Random Acts of Murder
#2 Random Acts of Deceit
#2.5 Random Acts of Scrooge
#3 Random Acts of Malice
#4 Random Acts of Greed
#5 Random Acts of Fraud

The Worst Detective Ever:

I'm not really a private detective. I just play one on TV.

Joey Darling, better known to the world as Raven Remington, detective extraordinaire, is trying to separate herself from her invincible alter ego. She played the spunky character for five years on the hit TV show *Relentless*, which catapulted her to fame and into the role of Hollywood's sweetheart. When her marriage falls apart, her finances dwindle to nothing, and her father disappears, Joey finds herself on the Outer Banks of North Carolina, trying to piece together her life away from the limelight. But as people continually mistake her for the character she played on TV, she's tasked with solving real life crimes . . . even though she's terrible at it.

#1 Ready to Fumble

The Worst Detective Ever:

About the Author

USA Today has called Christy Barritt's books "scary, funny, passionate, and quirky."

Christy writes both mystery and romantic suspense novels that are clean with underlying messages of faith. Her books have won the Daphne du Maurier Award for Excellence in Suspense and Mystery, have been twice nominated for the Romantic Times Reviewers' Choice Award, and have finaled for both a Carol Award and Foreword Magazine's Book of the Year.

She is married to her Prince Charming, a man who thinks she's hilarious—but only when she's not trying to be. Christy is a self-proclaimed klutz, an avid music lover who's known for spontaneously bursting into song, and a road trip aficionado.

When she's not working or spending time with her family, she enjoys singing, playing the guitar, and exploring small, unsuspecting towns where people have no idea how accident-prone she is.

Find Christy online at:

www.christybarritt.com
www.facebook.com/christybarritt
www.twitter.com/cbarritt

Sign up for Christy's newsletter to get information on all of her latest releases here: **www.christybarritt.com/newsletter-sign-up/**

If you enjoyed this book, please consider leaving a review.

Made in the USA
Coppell, TX
07 August 2021